Jerry Bauer

Sigrid Nunez is the author of the novels *For Rouenna* and *The Last of Her Kind*. She has received several awards, including a Whiting Writers' Award, the Rome Prize in Literature, and a Berlin Prize Fellowship. She lives in New York City.

Also by Sigrid Nunez

The Last of Her Kind
For Rouenna
Mitz: The Marmoset of Bloomsbury
Naked Sleeper

Additional Acclaim for
Sigrid Nunez's *A Feather on the Breath of God*

"An intelligent and poignant examination of social and erotic displacement, and written with such extraordinary and seemingly unstudied conviction that one accepts every word of it as truth."

—*The Atlantic Monthly*

"*A Feather on the Breath of God* brilliantly succeeds in describing a life on the fringe, outside the conventional categories of cultural and personal identity. . . . A remarkable book, full of strange brilliance, trembling with fury and tenderness."

—*The Philadelphia Inquirer*

"Nunez nearly transforms literature into ballet."

—*The Washington Post*

"Wise and beautiful. This novel is now on my favorite-books list."
—Carolyn Chute, author of *Snow Man*

"An exquisite novel that saves us from our primal fears of loss by reaffirming our belief in the immortality of love. The book is complex and beautifully felt, and I was haunted by it. Sigrid Nunez is a radiant and tenacious writer."

—Fae Myenne Ng, author of *Bone*

A Feather
on the
Breath of God

a novel by

Sigrid Nunez

Picador
Farrar, Straus and Giroux
New York

The author wishes to thank the Corporation of Yaddo, the MacDowell Colony, Blue Mountain Center, the Barbara Deming Memorial Fund, and the Mrs. Giles Whiting Foundation for their generous support.

www.picadorusa.com

Picador® is a U.S. registered trademark and is used by Farrar, Straus and Giroux under license from Pan Books Limited.

For information on Picador Reading Group Guides, as well as ordering, please contact Picador.
Phone: 646-307-5629
Fax: 212-253-9627
E-mail: readinggroupguides@picadorusa.com

Parts of this book were originally published, in slightly different form, in the *Threepenny Review* and the *Iowa Review*.

Designed by C. Linda Dingler

Library of Congress Cataloging-in-Publication Data

Nunez, Sigrid.
    A feather on the breath of God : a novel / Sigrid Nunez.
        p. cm.
    ISBN 0-312-42273-3
    EAN 978-0-312-42273-8
    1. Young women—New York (N.Y.)—Fiction. 2. Chinese Americans—New York (N.Y.)—Fiction. 3. German Americans—New York (N.Y.)—Fiction. 4. Ballet dancers—New York (N.Y.)—Fiction. 5. Family—New York (N.Y.)—Fiction. I. Title.

PS3564.U475F4 1995
                                                                              94-22766

First published in the United States by HarperCollins*Publishers*

First Picador Edition: January 2006

10 9 8 7 6 5 4 3 2 1

CHANG

The first time I ever heard my father speak Chinese was at Coney Island. I don't remember how old I was then, but I must have been very young. This was in the early days, when we still went on family outings. We were walking along the boardwalk when we ran into the four Chinese men. My mother told the story often, as if she thought we'd forgotten. "You kids didn't know them and neither did I. They were friends of your father's, from Chinatown. You'd never heard Chinese before. You didn't know what was up. You stood there with your mouths hanging open—I had to laugh. 'Why are they singing? Why is Daddy singing?'"

One of the men gave each of my sisters and me a dollar bill. I cashed mine into dimes and set out to win a goldfish. A dime bought you three chances to toss a Ping-Pong ball into one of many small fishbowls, each holding a quivering tangerine-colored fish. Overexcited, I threw recklessly, again and again. When all the dimes were gone I ran back to the grown-ups in tears. The man who had given me the dollar tried to give me another, but my parents wouldn't allow it.

He pressed the bag of peanuts he had been eating into my hands and said I could have them all.

I never saw any of those men again or heard anything about them. They were the only friends of my father's that I would ever meet. I would hear him speak Chinese again, but very seldom. In Chinese restaurants, occasionally on the telephone, once or twice in his sleep, and in the hospital when he was dying.

So it was true, then. He really was Chinese. Up until that day I had not quite believed it.

My mother always said that he had sailed to America on a boat. He took a slow boat from China, was what she used to say, laughing. I wasn't sure whether she was serious, and if she was, why coming from China was such a funny thing.

A slow boat from China. In time I learned that he was born not in China but in Panama. No wonder I only half-believed he was Chinese. He was only half-Chinese.

The facts I know about his life are unbearably few. Although we shared the same house for eighteen years, we had little else in common. We had no culture in common. It is only a slight exaggeration to say that we had no language in common. By the time I was born my father had lived almost thirty years in America, but to hear him speak you would not have believed this. About his failure to master English there always seemed to me something willful. Except for her accent—as thick as but so different from his—my mother had no such trouble.

"He never would talk about himself much, you know.

That was his way. He never really had much to say, in general. Silence was golden. It was a cultural thing, I think." (My mother.)

By the time I was old enough to understand this, my father had pretty much stopped talking.

Taciturnity: They say that is an Oriental trait. But I don't believe my father was always the silent, withdrawn man I knew. Think of that day at Coney Island, when he was talking a Chinese blue streak.

Almost everything I know about him came from my mother, and there was much she herself never knew, much she had forgotten or was unsure of, and much she would never tell.

I am six, seven, eight years old, a schoolgirl with deplorable posture and constantly cracked lips, chafing in the dollish Old World clothes handmade by my mother; a bossy, fretful, sly, cowardly child given to fits of temper and weeping. In school, or in the playground, or perhaps watching television, I hear something about the Chinese—something odd, improbable. I will ask my father. He will know whether it is true, say, that the Chinese eat with sticks.

He shrugs. He pretends not to understand. Or he scowls and says, "Chinese just like everybody else."

("He thought you were making fun of him. He always thought everyone was making fun of him. He had a chip on his shoulder. The way he acted, you'd've thought he was colored!")

Actually, he said "evvybody."

Is it true the Chinese write backwards?

Chinese just like evvybody else.

Is it true they eat dog?

Chinese just like evvybody else.

Are they really all Communists?

Chinese just like evvybody else.

What is Chinese water torture? What is foot-binding?
What is a mandarin?

Chinese just like evvybody else.

He was not like everybody else.

The unbearably few facts are these. He was born in Colón, Panama, in 1911. His father came from Shanghai. From what I have been able to gather, Grandfather Chang was a merchant engaged in the trade of tobacco and tea. This business, which he ran with one of his brothers, kept him traveling often between Shanghai and Colón. He had two wives, one in each city, and, as if out of a passion for symmetry, two sons by each wife. Soon after my father, Carlos, was born, his father took him to Shanghai, to be raised by the Chinese wife. Ten years later my father was sent back to Colón. I never understood the reason for this. The way the story was told to me, I got the impression that my father was being sent away from some danger. This was, of course, a time of upheaval in China, the decade following the birth of the Republic, the era of the warlords. If the date is correct, my father would have left Shanghai the year the Chinese Communist party was founded there. It remains uncertain, though, whether political events had anything at all to do with his leaving China.

One year after my father returned to Colón his mother

was dead. I remember hearing as a child that she had died of a stroke. Years later this would seem to me odd, when I figured out that she would have been only twenty-six. Odder still, to think of that reunion between the long-parted mother and son; there's a good chance they did not speak the same language. The other half-Panamanian son, Alfonso, was either sent back with my father or had never left Colón. After their mother's death the two boys came into the care of their father's brother and business partner, Uncle Mee, who apparently lived in Colón and had a large family of his own.

Grandfather Chang, his Chinese wife, and their two sons remained in Shanghai. All were said to have been killed by the Japanese. That must have been during the Sino-Japanese War. My father would have been between his late twenties and early thirties by then, but whether he ever saw any of those Shanghai relations again before they died, I don't know.

At twelve or thirteen my father sailed to America with Uncle Mee. I believe it was just the two of them who came, leaving the rest of the family in Colón. Sometime in the next year or so my father was enrolled in a public school in Brooklyn. I remember coming across a notebook that had belonged to him in those days and being jolted by the name written on the cover: Charles Cipriano Chang. That was neither my father's first nor his last name, as far as I knew, and I'd never heard of the middle name. (Hard to believe that my father spent his boyhood in Shanghai being called Carlos, a name he could not even pronounce with the proper Spanish accent. So he must have had a Chinese name as well. And although our family never knew this name, perhaps among Chinese people he used it.)

Twenty years passed. All I know about this part of my father's life is that it was lived illegally in New York, mostly in Chinatown, where he worked in various restaurants. Then came the Second World War and he was drafted. It was while he was in the army that he finally became an American citizen. He was no longer calling himself Charles but Carlos again, and now, upon becoming a citizen, he dropped his father's family name and took his mother's. Why a man who thought of himself as Chinese, who had always lived among Chinese, who spoke little Spanish, and who had barely known his mother would have made such a decision in the middle of his life is one of many mysteries surrounding my father.

My mother had an explanation. "You see, Alfonso was a Panamanian citizen, and *he* had taken his mother's name" (which would, of course, be in keeping with Spanish cultural tradition). "He was the only member of his family your father had left—the others were all dead. Your father wanted to have the same last name as his brother. Also, he thought he'd get along better in this country with a Spanish name." This makes no sense to me. He'd been a Chinatown Chang for twenty years. Now all of a sudden he wished to pass for Hispanic?

In another version of this story, the idea of getting rid of the Chinese name was attributed to the citizenship official handling my father's papers. This is plausible, given that immigration restrictions for Chinese were still in effect at that time. But I have not ruled out the possibility that the change of names was the result of a misunderstanding between my father and this official. My father was an easily fuddled man, especially when dealing with authority, and he always had trouble understanding and making himself understood in English. And I can imagine him not only befuddled enough to make such a mistake but also too timid afterward to try to fix it.

Whatever really happened I'm sure I'll never know. I do know that having a Spanish name brought much confusion into my father's life and have always wondered in what way my own life might have been different had he kept the name Chang.

From this point on the story becomes somewhat clearer.

With the Hundredth Infantry Division my father goes to war, fights in France and Germany, and, after V-E Day, is stationed in the small southern German town where he will meet my mother. He is thirty-four and she has just turned eighteen. She is soon pregnant.

Here is rich food for speculation: How did they communicate? She had had a little English in school. He learned a bit of German. They must have misunderstood far more than they understood of each other. Perhaps this helps to explain why my eldest sister was already two and my other sister on the way before my parents got married. (My sisters and I did not learn about this until we were in our twenties.)

By the time I was three they would already have had two long separations.

"I should have married Rudolf!" (My mother.)

Nineteen forty-eight. My father returns to the States with his wife and first daughter. Now everything is drastically changed. A different America this: the America of the citizen, the legal worker, the family man. No more drinking and gambling till all hours in Chinatown. No more drifting from job to job, living hand to mouth, sleeping on the floor of a friend's room or on a shelf in the restaurant kitchen. There are new, undreamed-of expenses: household money, layettes, taxes, insurance, a special bank account for the children's education. He does the best he can. He rents an apartment in the Fort Greene housing project, a short walk from the Cantonese restaurant on Fulton Street where he works as a waiter. Some nights after closing, after all the tables have been cleared and the dishes done, he stays for the gambling. He weaves home to a wide-awake wife who sniffs the whiskey on his breath and doesn't care whether he has lost or won. So little money—to gamble with any of it is a sin. Her English is getting better ("no thanks to him!"), but for what she has to say she needs little vocabulary. She is miserable. She hates America. She dreams incessantly about going home. There is something peculiar about the three-year-old: She rarely smiles; she claws at the pages of magazines, like a cat. The one-year-old is prone to colic. To her horror my mother learns that she is pregnant again. She attempts an abortion, which fails. I am born. About that attempt, was my father consulted? Most likely not. Had he been I think I know what he would have said. He would have said: No, this time it will be a boy. Like most men he would have wanted a son. (All girls—a house full of females—a Chinese man's nightmare!) Perhaps with a son he would have been more open. Perhaps a son he would have taught Chinese.

He gets another job, as a dishwasher in the kitchen of a large public health service hospital. He will work there until he retires, eventually being promoted to kitchen supervisor.

He moves his family to another housing project, outside the city, newly built, cleaner, safer.

He works all the time. On weekends, when he is off from the hospital, he waits on tables in one or another Chinese restaurant. He works most holidays and takes no vacation. On his rare day off he outrages my mother by going to the racetrack. But he is not self-indulgent. A little gambling, a quart of Budweiser with his supper—eaten alone, an hour or so after the rest of us (he always worked late)—now and then a glass of Scotch, cigarettes—these were his only pleasures. While the children are still small there are occasional outings. To Coney Island, Chinatown, the zoo. On Sundays sometimes he takes us to the children's matinee, and once a year to Radio City, for the Christmas or Easter show. But he and my mother never go out alone together, just the two of them—never.

Her English keeps getting better, making his seem worse and worse.

He is hardly home, yet my memory is of constant fighting.

Not much vocabulary needed to wound.

"Stupid woman. Crazy lady. Talk, talk, talk, talk—never say nothing!"

"I should have married Rudolf!"

Once, she spat in his face. Another time, she picked up a bread knife and he had to struggle to get it away from her.

They slept in separate beds.

Every few months she announced to the children that it

was over: We were going "home." (And she did go back with us to Germany once, when I was two. We stayed six months. About this episode she was always vague. In years to come, whenever we asked her why we did not stay in Germany, she would say, "You children wanted your father." But I think that is untrue. More likely she realized that there was no life for her back there. She had never gotten on well with her family. By this time I believe Rudolf had married another.)

Even working the two jobs, my father did not make much money. He would never make enough to buy a house. Yet it seemed the burden of being poor weighed heavier on my mother. Being poor meant you could never relax, meant eternal attention to appearances. Just because you had no money didn't mean you were squalid. Come into the house: See how clean and tidy everything is. Look at the children: spotless. And people did comment to my mother—on the shininess of her floors and how she kept her children—and she was gratified by this. Still, being poor was exhausting.

One day a woman waist-deep in children knocked at the door. When my mother answered, the woman apologized. "I thought—from the name on the mailbox I thought you were Spanish too. My kids needed to use the toilet." My mother could not hide her displeasure. She was proud of being German, and in those postwar years she was also bitterly defensive. When people called us names—spicks and chinks—she said, "You see how it is in this country. For all they say how bad we Germans are, no one ever calls you names for being German."

She had no patience with my father's quirks. The involuntary twitching of a muscle meant that someone had given him the evil eye. Drinking a glass of boiled water while it was still hot cured the flu. He saved back issues of *Reader's Digest* and silver dollars from certain years, believing that one day they'd be worth a lot of money. What sort of backward creature had she married? His English drove her mad. Whenever he didn't catch something that was said to him (and this happened all the time), instead of saying "What?" he said "Who?" "Who? Who?" she screeched back at him. "What are you, an owl?"

Constant bickering and fighting.

We children dreamed of growing up, going to college, getting married, getting away.

And what about Alfonso and Uncle Mee? What happened to them?

"I never met either of them, but we heard from Mee all the time those first years—it was awful. By then he was back in Panama. He was a terrible gambler, and so were his sons. They had debts up to here—and who should they turn to but your father. Uncle What-About-Mee, I called him. 'Think of all I've done for you. You owe me.'" (And though she had never heard it she mimicked his voice.) "Well, your father had managed to save a couple of thousand dollars and he sent it all to Mee. I could have died. I never forgave him. I was pregnant then, and I had one maternity dress—one. Mee no sooner got that money than he wrote back for more. I told your father if he sent him another dime I was leaving."

Somehow the quarrel extended to include Alfonso, who seems to have sided with Mee. My father broke with them both. Several years after we left Brooklyn, an ad appeared in the Chinatown newspaper. Alfonso and Mee were trying to track my father down. He never answered the ad, my father said. He never spoke to either man again. (Perhaps he lied. Perhaps he was always in touch with them, secretly. I believe much of his life was a secret from us.)

I have never seen a photograph of my father that was taken before he was in the army. I have no idea what he looked like as a child or as a young man. I have never seen any photographs of his parents or his brothers, or of Uncle Mee, or of any other relations, or of the houses he lived in in Colón or Shanghai. If my father had any possessions that had belonged to his parents, any family keepsakes or mementos of his youth, I never saw them. About his youth he had nothing to tell. A single anecdote he shared with me. In Shanghai he had a dog. When my father sailed to Panama, the dog was brought along to the dock to see him off. My father boarded the boat and the dog began howling. He never forgot that: the boat pulling away from the dock and the dog howling. "Dog no fool. He know I never be back."

In our house there were no Chinese things. No objects made of bamboo or jade. No lacquer boxes. No painted scrolls or fans. No calligraphy. No embroidered silks. No Buddhas. No chopsticks among the silverware, no rice bowls or tea sets. No Chinese tea, no ginseng or soy sauce in the cupboards. My father was the only Chinese thing, sitting like a Buddha himself among the Hummels and cuckoo clocks and pictures of Alpine landscapes. My mother thought of the house as hers, spoke of *her* curtains, *her* floors (often in warning: "Don't scuff up my floors!") The daughters were hers too. To each of them she gave a Nordic name, impossible for him to pronounce. ("*What* does your father call you?" That question—an agony to me—rang through my childhood.) It was part of her abiding nostalgia that she wanted to raise her children as Germans. She sewed dirndls for them and even for their dolls. She braided their hair, then wound the braids tightly around their ears, like hair earmuffs, in the German style. They would open their presents on Christmas Eve rather than Christmas morning. They would not celebrate Thanksgiving. Of course they would not celebrate any Chinese holiday. No dragon and firecrackers on Chinese New Year's. For Christmas there was red cabbage and sauerbraten. Imagine my father saying *sauerbraten.*

Now and then he brought home food from Chinatown: fiery red sausage with specks of fat like embedded teeth, dried fish, buns filled with bean paste that he cracked us up by calling *Chinese pee-nus butter.* My mother would not touch any of it. ("God knows what it really is.") We kids clamored for a taste and when we didn't like it my father got angry. ("You know how he was with that chip on his shoulder. He took it personally. He was insulted.") Whenever we ate at one of the restaurants where he worked, he was always careful to order for us the same Americanized dishes served to most of the white customers.

An early memory: I am four, five, six years old, in a silly mood, mugging in my mother's bureau mirror. My father is in the room with me but I forget he is there. I place my forefingers at the corners of my eyes and pull the lids taut. Then I catch him watching me. His is a look of pure hate.

"He thought you were making fun."

A later memory: "Panama is an isthmus." Grade-school geography. My father looks up from his paper, alert, suspicious. "Merry Isthmus!" "Isthmus be the place!" My sisters and I shriek with laughter. My father shakes his head. "Not nice, making fun of place where people born!"

"Ach, he had no sense of humor—he never did. He never got the point of a joke."

It is true I hardly ever heard him laugh. (Unlike my mother, who, despite her chronic unhappiness, seemed always to be laughing—at him, at us, at the neighbors. A great tease she was, sly, malicious, often witty.)

Chinese inscrutability. Chinese sufferance. Chinese reserve. Yes, I recognize my father in the clichés. But what about his Panamanian side? What are Latins said to be? Hot-blooded, mercurial, soulful, macho, convivial, romantic, rash. No, he was none of these.

"He always wanted to go back. He always missed China."

But he was only ten years old when he left.

"Yes, but that's what counts—where you spent those first years, and your first language. That's who you are."

I had a children's book about Sun Yat Sen, the Man Who Changed China. There were drawings of Sun as a boy. I tried to picture my father like that, a Chinese boy who wore pajamas outdoors and a coolie hat and a pigtail down his back. (Though of course in those days after Sun's revolution he isn't likely to have worn a pigtail.) I pictured my father against those landscapes of peaks and pagodas, with a dog like Old Yeller at his heels. What was it like, this boyhood in Shanghai? How did the Chinese wife treat the second wife's son? (My father and Alfonso would not have had the same status as the official wife's sons, I don't think.) How did the Chinese brothers treat him? When he went to school—did he go to school?—was he accepted by the other children as one of them? Is there a Chinese word for half-breed, and was he called that name as we would be? Surely many times in his life he must have wished that he were all Chinese. My mother wished that her children were all German. I wanted to be an all-American girl with a name like Sue Brown.

He always wanted to go back.

He never forgot that dog howling on the dock.

In our house there were not many books. My mother's romances and historical novels, books about Germany (mostly about the Nazi era), a volume of Shakespeare, tales from Andersen and Grimm, the *Nibelungenlied*, Edith Hamilton's *Mythology*, works of Goethe and Heine, *Struwwelpeter*, the drawings of Wilhelm Busch. It was my mother who gave me that book about Sun Yat Sen and, when I was a little older, one of her own favorites, *The Good Earth*, a children's story for adults. Pearl Buck was a missionary who lived in China for many years. (Missionaries supposedly converted the Changs to Christianity. From what? Buddhism? Taoism? My father's mother was almost certainly Roman Catholic. He himself belonged to no

church.) Pearl Buck wrote eighty-four books, founded a
shelter for Asian-American children, and won the Nobel
Prize.

The Good Earth. China a land of famine and plagues—
endless childbirth among them. The births of daughters
seen as evil omens. "It is only a slave this time—not worth
mentioning." Little girls sold as a matter of course.
Growing up to be concubines with names like Lotus and
Cuckoo and Pear Blossom. Women with feet like little
deer hooves. Abject wives, shuffling six paces behind their
men. All this filled me with anxiety. In our house the husband was the meek and browbeaten one.

I never saw my father read, except for the newspaper.
He did not read the *Reader's Digest*s that he saved. He would
not have been able to read *The Good Earth.* I am sure he
could not write with fluency in any tongue. The older I
grew the more I thought of him as illiterate. Hard for me
to accept the fact that he did not read books. Say I grew
up to be a writer. He would not read what I wrote.

He had his own separate closet, in the front hall.
Every night when he came home from work he undressed
as soon as he walked in, out there in the hall. He took
off his suit and put on his bathrobe. He always wore a
suit to work, but at the hospital he changed into whites
and at the restaurant into dark pants, white jacket, and
black bow tie. In the few photographs of him that exist
he is often wearing a uniform—his soldier's or hospital-
worker's or waiter's.

Though not at all vain, he was particular about his
appearance. He bought his suits in a men's fine clothing

store on Fifth Avenue, and he took meticulous care of them. He had a horror of cheap cloth and imitation leather, and an equal horror of slovenliness. His closet was the picture of order. On the top shelf, where he kept his hats, was a large assortment—a lifetime's supply, it seemed to me—of chewing gum, cough drops, and mints. On that shelf he kept also his cigarettes and cigars. The closet smelled much as he did—of tobacco and spearmint and the rosewater-glycerin cream he used on his dry skin. A not unpleasant smell.

He was small. At fourteen I was already as tall as he, and eventually I would outweigh him. A trim sprig of a man, dainty but not puny, fastidious but not effeminate. I used to marvel at the cleanliness of his nails, and at his good teeth, which never needed any fillings. By the time I was born he had lost most of his top hair, which made his domed forehead look even larger, his moon face rounder. It may have been the copper-red cast of his skin that led some people to take him for an American Indian—people who'd never seen one, probably.

He could be cruel. I once saw him blow pepper in the cat's face. He loathed that cat, a surly, untrainable tom found in the street. But he was very fond of another creature we took in, an orphaned nestling sparrow. Against expectations, the bird survived and learned to fly. But, afraid that it would not know how to fend for itself outdoors, we decided to keep it. My father sometimes sat by its cage, watching the bird and cooing to it in Chinese. My mother was amused. "You see: He has more to say to that bird than to us!" The emperor and his nightingale, she

called them. "The Chinese have always loved their birds."
(What none of us knew: At that very moment in China keeping pet birds had been prohibited as a bourgeois affectation, and sparrows were being exterminated as pests.)

It was true that my father had less and less to say to us. He was drifting further and further out of our lives. These were my teenage years. I did not see clearly what was happening then, and for long afterward, whenever I tried to look back, a panic would come over me, so that I couldn't see at all.

At sixteen, I had stopped thinking about becoming a writer. I wanted to dance. Every day after school I went into the city for class. I would be home by eight-thirty, about the same time as my father, and so for this period he and I would eat dinner together. And much later, looking back, I realized that was when I had—and lost—my chance. Alone with my father every night, I could have gotten to know him. I could have asked him all those questions that I now have to live without answers to. Of course he would have resisted talking about himself. But with patience I might have drawn him out.

Or maybe not. As I recall, the person sitting across the kitchen table from me was like a figure in a glass case. That was not the face of someone thinking, feeling, or even daydreaming. It was the clay face, still waiting to receive the breath of life.

If it ever occurred to me that my father was getting old, that he was exhausted, that his health was failing, I don't remember it.

He was still working seven days a week. Sometimes he

missed having dinner with me because the dishwasher broke and he had to stay late at the hospital. For a time, on Saturdays, he worked double shifts and did not come home till we were all asleep.

After dinner, he stayed at the kitchen table, smoking and finishing his beer. He never joined the rest of us in the living room in front of the television. He sat alone at the table, staring at the wall. He hardly noticed if someone came into the kitchen for something. His inobservance was the family's biggest joke. My mother would give herself or one of us a new hairdo and say, "Now watch: Your father won't even notice," and she was right.

My sisters and I bemoaned his stubborn avoidance of the living room. Once a year he yielded and joined us around the Christmas tree, but only very reluctantly; we had to beg him.

I knew vaguely that he continued to have some sort of social life outside the house, a life centered in Chinatown.

He still played the horses.

By this time family outings had ceased. We never did anything together as a family.

But every Sunday my father came home with ice cream for everyone.

He and my mother fought less and less—seldom now in the old vicious way—but this did not mean there was peace. Never any word or gesture of affection between them, not even, "for the sake of the children," pretense of affection.

(Television: the prime-time family shows. During the inevitable scenes when family love and loyalty were affirmed, the discomfort in the living room was palpable. I think we were all ashamed of how far below the ideal our family fell.)

Working and saving to send his children to college, he took no interest in their school life. He did, however, reward good report cards with cash. He did not attend school events to which parents were invited; he always had to work.

He never saw me dance.

He intrigued my friends, who angered me by regarding him as if he were a figure in a glass case. Doesn't he ever come out of the kitchen? Doesn't he ever talk? I was angry at him too, for what he seemed to be doing: *willing* himself into stereotype—inscrutable, self-effacing, funny little Chinaman.

And why couldn't he learn to speak English?

He developed the tight wheezing cough that would never leave him. The doctor blamed cigarettes, so my father tried sticking to cigars. The cough was particularly bad at night. It kept my mother up, and she started sleeping on the living-room couch.

I was the only one who went to college, and I got a scholarship. My father gave the money he had saved to my mother, who bought a brand-new Mercedes, the family's first car.

He was not like everybody else. In fact, he was not like anyone I had ever met. But I thought of my father when I first encountered the "little man" of Russian literature. I thought of him a lot when I read the stories of Chekhov and Gogol. Reading "Grief," I remembered my father and the sparrow, and a new possibility presented itself: my father not as one who would not speak but as one to whom no one would listen.

And he was like a character in a story also in the sense that he needed to be invented.

The silver dollars saved in a cigar box. The *Reader's Digest*s going back to before I was born. The uniforms. The tobacco-mint-rosewater smell. I cannot invent a father out of these.

I waited too long. By the time I started gathering material for his story, whatever there had been in the way of private documents or papers (and there must have been some) had disappeared. (It was never clear whether my father himself destroyed them or whether my mother later lost or got rid of them, between moves, or in one of her zealous spring cleanings.)

The Sunday-night ice cream. The Budweiser bottle sweating on the kitchen table. The five-, ten-, or twenty-dollar bill he pulled from his wallet after squinting at your report card. "Who? Who?"

We must have seemed as alien to him as he seemed to us. To him we must always have been "others." Females. Demons. No different from other demons, who could not tell one Asian from another, who thought Chinese food meant chop suey and Chinese customs were matter for joking. I would have to live a lot longer and he would have to die before the full horror of this would sink in. And then it would sink in deeply, agonizingly, like an arrow that has found its mark.

➤

Dusk in the city. Dozens of Chinese men bicycle through the streets, bearing cartons of fried dumplings, Ten Ingredients Lo Mein, and sweet-and-sour pork. I am on my way to the drugstore when one of them hails me. "Miss! Wait, miss!" Not a man, I see, but a boy, eighteen at most, with a lovely, oval, fresh-skinned face. "You—you Chinese!" It is not the first time in my life this has happened. In as few words as possible, I explain. The boy turns out to have arrived just weeks ago, from Hong Kong. His English is incomprehensible. He is flustered when he finds I cannot speak Chinese. He says, "Can I. Your father. Now." It takes me a moment to figure this out. Alas, he is asking to meet my father. Unable to bring myself to tell him my father is dead, I say that he does not live in the city. The boy persists. "But sometime come see. And then I now?" His imploring manner puzzles me. Is it that he wants to meet Chinese people? Doesn't he work in a Chinese restaurant? Doesn't he know about Chinatown? I feel a surge of anxiety. He is so earnest and intent. I am missing something. In another minute I have promised that when my father comes to town he will go to the restaurant where the boy works and seek him out. The boy rides off looking pleased, and I continue on to the store. I am picking out toothpaste when he appears at my side. He hands me a folded piece of paper. Two telephone numbers and a message in Chinese characters. "For father."

He was sixty when he retired from the hospital, but his working days were not done. He took a part-time job as a messenger for a bank. That Christmas when I came home from school I found him in bad shape. His smoker's cough was much worse, and he had pains in his legs and in his back, recently diagnosed as arthritis.

But it was not smoker's cough, and it was not arthritis.

A month later, he left work early one day because he was in such pain. He made it to the station, but when he tried to board the train he could not get up the steps. Two conductors had to carry him on. At home he went straight to bed and in the middle of the night he woke up coughing as usual, and this time there was blood.

His decline was so swift that by the time I arrived at the hospital he barely knew me. Over the next week we were able to chart the backward journey on which he was embarked by his occasional murmurings. ("I got to get back to the base—they'll think I'm AWOL!") Though I was not there to hear it, I am told that he cursed my mother and accused her of never having cared. By the end of the week, when he spoke it was only in Chinese.

One morning a priest arrived. No one had sent for him. He had doubtless assumed from the name that this patient was Hispanic and Catholic, and had taken it upon himself to administer Extreme Unction. None of us had the will to stop him, and so we were witness to a final mystery: my father, who as far as we knew had no religion, feebly crossing himself.

The fragments of Chinese stopped. There was only panting then, broken by sharp gasps such as a person makes when reminded of some important thing he has forgotten. To the end his hands were restless. He kept repeating the same gesture: cupping his hands together and drawing them to his chest, as though gathering something to him.

Now let others speak.

"After the war was a terrible time. We were all scared to

death, we didn't know what was going to happen to us. Some of those soldiers were really enjoying it, they wanted nothing better than to see us grovel. The victors! Oh, they were scum, a lot of them. But your father felt sorry for us. He tried to help. And not just our family but the neighbors too. He gave us money. His wallet was always out. And he was always bringing stuff from the base, like coffee and chocolate—things you could never get. And even after he went back to the States he sent packages. Not just to us but to all the people he got to know here. Frau Meyer. The Schweitzers. They still talk about that." (My grandmother.)

"We know the cancer started in the right lung but by the time we saw him it had spread. It was in both lungs, it was in his liver and in his bones. He was a very sick man, and he'd been sick for a long time. I'd say that tumor in the right lung had been growing for at least five years." (The doctor.)

"He drank a lot in those days, and your mother didn't like that. But he was funny. He loved that singer—the cowboy—what was his name? I forget. Anyway, he put on the music and he sang along. Your mother would cover her ears." (My grandmother.)

"I didn't like the way he looked. He wouldn't say anything but I knew he was hurting. I said to myself, this isn't arthritis—no way. I wanted him to see my own doctor but he wouldn't. I was just about to order him to." (My father's boss at the bank.)

"He hated cats, and the cat knew it and she was always jumping in his lap. Every time he sat down the cat jumped in his lap and we laughed. But you could tell it really bothered him. He said cats were bad luck. When the cat jumped in your lap it was a bad omen." (My mother's younger brother Karl.)

"He couldn't dance at all—or he wouldn't—but he clapped and sang along to the records. He liked to drink and he liked gambling. Your mother worried about that." (Frau Meyer.)

"Before the occupation no one in this town had ever seen an Oriental or a Negro." (My grandmother.)

"He never ate much, he didn't want you to cook for him, but he liked German beer. He brought cigarettes for everyone. We gave him schnapps. He played us the cowboy songs." (Frau Schweitzer.)

"Ain't you people dying to know what he's saying?" (The patient in the bed next to my father's.)

"When he wasn't drinking he was very shy. He just sat there next to your mother without speaking. He sat there staring and staring at her." (Frau Meyer.)

"He liked blonds. He loved that blond hair." (Karl.)

"There was absolutely nothing we could do for him. The amazing thing is that he was working right up till the day he came into the hospital. I don't know how he did that." (The doctor.)

"The singing was a way of talking to us, because he didn't know German at all." (My grandmother.)

"Yes, of course I remember. It was Hank Williams. He played those records over and over. Hillbilly music. I thought I'd go mad." (My mother.)

Here are the names of some Hank Williams songs:
Honky Tonkin'. Ramblin' Man. Hey, Good Lookin'.

Lovesick Blues. Why Don't You Love Me Like You Used To Do. Your Cheatin' Heart. (I heard that) Lonesome Whistle. Why Don't You Mind Your Own Business. I'm So Lonesome I Could Cry. The Blues Come Around. Cold, Cold Heart. I'll Never Get Out of This World Alive. I Can't Help It If I'm Still in Love With You.

CHRISTA

I am told that my first word was *Coca-Cola,* and there exists a snapshot of me at eighteen months, running in a park, hugging a full bottle. It seems I snatched this Coke from some neighboring picnickers. I used to believe that I could remember this moment—the cold bottle against my stomach, my teetering, stomping trot, feelings of slyness and joy and excitement fizzing in me—but now I think I imagined all this at a later age, after having looked long and often at the picture.

Here is something I do remember. Coming home from grade school for the lunch hour: It may have happened only once or it may have happened every day. Part of the way home took me through empty streets. I was alone and afraid. The noon whistle sounded, and as at a signal I started to run. The drumming of my feet and my own huffing breath became someone or something behind me. And I remember thinking that if I could just get home to my mother and her blue, blue eyes, everything would be all right.

Here are some lines from Virginia Woolf: ". . . there is nothing to take the place of childhood. A leaf of mint brings it back: or a cup with a blue ring."

Sometimes—now—I might find myself in a strange town. I might be walking down a quiet street at midday. A factory whistle blows, and I feel a current in my blood, as if a damp sponge had been stroked down my back.

Woolf was thinking of a happy childhood, but does it matter? Another writer, members of whose family were killed in concentration camps, recalls how years later, looking through a book, he was touched by photographs of Hitler, because they reminded him of his childhood.

My mother's eyes were enhanced by shapely brows that made me think of angels' wings. Their arch gave her face an expression of skeptical wonder. When she was displeased her brows went awry; the arch fell; the world came tumbling down on me.

I remember a pear-shaped bottle of shampoo that sat on the edge of our bathtub. "With lemon juice. For blonds only." As the years passed and her hair grew darker, she started to use bleach. On the smooth white drawing paper of kindergarten I too made her blonder, choosing the bright yellow crayon, the yellow of spring flowers: daffodils, forsythia.

Other features: A wide mouth. Good, clear skin. A strong nose. Too big, her daughters said. ("What do you mean? A fine nose. Aristocratic. Same nose as Queen Elizabeth. I don't want a little button on my face.")

And her walk, which was graceful and not graceful. A slight hitch in her gait, like a dancer with an injury.

And her hands: Long-fingered, with soft palms and squarish nails. Deft, competent hands, good at making things.

This is the way I see her at first, not as a whole but as

parts: a pair of hands, a pair of eyes. Two colors: yellow and blue.

The housing project where we lived. The wooden benches that stood in front of each building, where the women gathered when the weather was fair. The women: mothers all, still in their twenties but already somewhat worn away. The broad spread of their bottoms. The stony hardness of their feet, thrust into flip-flops. (The slatternly sound of those flip-flops as they walked.) The hard lives of housewives without money. Exhaustion pooled under their eyes and in their veiny ankles. One or two appearing regularly in sunglasses to hide a black eye.

Talking, smoking, filing their nails.

Time passes. The shadow of the building lengthens. The first stars come out; the mosquitoes. The children edge closer, keeping mum so as not to be chased away, not to miss a riddle. "He married his mother." "I'm late this month." "She lost the baby." "She found a lump." "She had a boy in the bed with her."

Finally a husband throws open a window. "Youse girls gonna yak out there the whole damn night?"

Part of my way of seeing my mother is in contrast to these women. It was part of the way she saw herself. "I'm not like these American women." Her boast that she spoke a better English than they was true. "*Dese* and *dose, youse, ain't.* How can you treat your own language like that!" Her own grammar was good, her spelling perfect, her handwriting precise, beautiful. But she made mistakes too. She said *spedacular* and *expecially* and *holier-than-thoo.* She spoke of a *bone of contentment* between two people. Accused someone of being a *ne'er-too-well*. And: "They stood in a motel for a week." No matter how many times you corrected her she could not get that verb right. She flapped her hands. "You know what I mean!" And her accent never changed. There were times when she had to repeat herself to a puzzled waitress or salesman.

But she would never say *youse*. She would never say *ain't*.

Parent-Teachers' Day. My mother comes home with a face set in disgust. "Your teacher said, 'She does *good* in history.'"

My mother liked English. "A good language—same family as German." She was capable of savoring a fine Anglo-Saxon word: *murky, smite*. She read *Beowulf* and *The Canterbury Tales*. She knew words like *thane* and *rood* and *sith*.

Southern drawls, heartland twangs, black English, all sounded horrid to her.

One or two Briticisms had found their way (how?) into her speech. "It was a proper mess, I tell you." And somewhere she had learned to swear. She had her own rules. Only the lowest sort of person would say *fuck*. But *bastard* was permissible. And *shit*—she said *shit* a lot. But she always sounded ridiculous, swearing. She called her daughters *sons of bitches*. I was never so aware that English was not her native tongue as when she was swearing at me.

She did not have many opportunities to speak German. We had a few relations, in upstate New York and in Pennsylvania, and there was a woman named Aga, from Munich, who had been my mother's first friend here in the States and who now lived in Yonkers. But visits with these people were rare, and perhaps that is why I first thought of German as a festive language, a language for special occasions. The harshness that grates on so many non-German ears—I never heard that. When several people were speaking together, it sounded to me like a kind of music—music that was not melodious, but full of jangles and toots and rasps, like a wind-up toy band.

From time to time we took the bus across town to a delicatessen owned by a man originally from Bremen. My mother ordered in German, and while the man was weighing and wrapping the Leberkäse and Blutwurst and ham, he and she would talk. But I was usually outside playing with the dachshund.

Sometimes, reading German poetry, she would start to say the lines under her breath. Then it no longer sounded like music, but like a dream-language: seething, urgent, a little scary.

She did not want to teach her children German. "It's not your language, you don't need it, learn your own language first."

Now and then, on television, in a war movie, say, an American actor would deliver some German lines, and my mother would hoot. If subtitles were used, she said they were wrong. When my elder sister took German in high school, my mother skimmed her textbook and threw it down. "Ach, so many things wrong!"

A very hard thing it seemed, getting German right.

In one of my own schoolbooks was a discussion of different peoples and the contributions each had made to American society. The Germans, who gave us Wernher von Braun, were described as being, among other things, obedient to authority, with a tendency to follow orders without questioning them. That gave me pause. I could not imagine my mother taking orders from anyone.

I remember being teased in school for the way I said certain words. *Stoomach.* And: "I stood outside all day." ("Musta got awful tired!") I called the sideways colon the Germans put on top of certain vowels an *omelette.* Later, after I'd left home, I had only to hear a snatch of German, or to see some Gothic script, to have my childhood come surging back to me.

My mother said, "English is a fine language, it gets you to most places that you want to go. But German is— deeper, I think. A better language for poetry. A more romantic language, better for describing—yearning."

Her favorite poet was Heine.

She said, "There are a lot of German words for which you have no English. And it's funny—so often it's an important word, one that means such a lot. *Weltschmerz.* How can you translate that? And even if you study German, you can't ever really learn a word like that, you never grasp what it means."

But I did learn it, and I think I know what *Weltschmerz* means.

My first book was a translation from the German: fairy tales of the Brothers Grimm. My mother read these stories aloud to me, before I had learned to read myself. What appealed to me was not so much the adventures, not the morals, but the details: a golden key, an emerald box, boots of buffalo leather. The strangeness and beauty of names like Gretel and Rapunzel, especially the way my mother said them. The notion of enchantment was a tangled one. You couldn't always believe what you saw. The twelve pigeons pecking on the lawn might be twelve princes under a spell. Perhaps all that was lacking in one's own household was the right magic. At the right word, one of those birds might fly to your hand bearing in his beak a golden key, and that key might open a door leading to who knew what treasure. My mother shared this with all her neighbors: the conviction that we did not belong in the housing project. Out on the benches, much of the talk was about getting out. It was all a mistake. We were all under a spell—the spell of poverty. What is a home? We project children drew pictures of houses with peaked roofs and chimneys, and yards with trees. My mother said, "Every decent family is getting out," as one by one our neighbors moved away. "We'll never get out, we'll be the last ones left," meaning: the last white family.

Metamorphosis. First the fairy tales, then the Greek myths—for years my imagination fed on that most magical possibility: a person could be changed into a creature, a tree. In time this led to trouble.

I can still see her, Mrs. Wynn, a twig of a woman with a long chin and hollow eyes: my teacher. The way my mother mimicked her, Mrs. Wynn became a witch from one of the stories. "Your daughter says, In my first life I was a rabbit, in my second life, I was a tree. I think she is too old to be telling stories like that." And then my mother, mimicking herself, all wide-blue-eyed innocence: "How do you know she wasn't a rabbit?"

Oh, how I loved her.

Because my mother gave it to me I read a book of German sagas, but I didn't like them. Heroism on the fierce Nordic scale was not for me. To Siegfried I preferred the heroes of the *Hausmärchen:* simple Hanses, farmers and tailors and their faithful horses and dogs. (In a few more years I'd prefer to read only about horses and dogs.) I did not share her taste for the legends of chivalry or the romances of the Middle Ages. The epic was her form. She liked stories—legendary or historic—about heroic striving, conquest and empire, royal houses and courts. Lives of Alexander and Napoleon were some of her favorite reading. (This was a mother who for Halloween dressed up her youngest not as a gypsy or a drum majorette but as Great Caesar's Ghost—pillowcase toga, philodendron wreath— stumping all the kids and not a few of the teachers.) She read piles of paperback romances too—what she called her "everyday" reading.

One day I came home to find her with a copy of *Lolita.* The woman who lived downstairs had heard it was a good dirty book and had gone out and bought it. Disappointed, she passed it on to my mother. ("So, is it dirty?" "No, just a very silly book by a very clever man.")

The "good" books, the ones to be kept, were placed in no particular order in a small pine bookcase whose top shelf was reserved for plants. To get at certain ones you had to part vines. Dear to my mother's heart was the legend of Faust. Goethe's version was years beyond me, but what I gathered of the story was not promising. I liked stories about the Devil all right, but Faust's ambition struck no chord in me. I was a child of limited curiosity. I wanted to hear the cat speak but I didn't care how it was done. Knowledge equals power was an empty formula to me. I was never good at science.

Shakespeare in one volume. Plutarch's *Lives,* abridged. In the introduction to the plays, I read that Shakespeare had used Plutarch as a source. At first I thought I had misunderstood. Then I felt a pang: The world was smaller than I had thought it was. For some reason, this gave me pain.

I remember a book given to me by my fourth-grade teacher. A thick, dark green, grainy cover, pleasant to touch. A story about immigrants. One man speaking to another of a young woman just arrived from the Old Country. The phrase stayed with me, along with the memory of the feelings it inspired. I was both moved and repelled. "She has still her mother's milk upon her lips."

My mother never called it the Old Country. She said *my country,* or *Germany,* or *home.* Usually *home.* When she spoke of home, I gave her my full attention. I could hear over and over (I did hear over and over) stories about her life *before*—before she was a wife, before she was Mother, when she was just Christa.

She was a good storyteller. To begin with, she spoke English with the same vigor and precision with which German is spoken. And she used everything—eyes, hands, all the muscles of her face. She was a good mimic, it was spooky how she became the person mimicked, and if that person was you, you got a taste of hell.

She was the opposite of my father. She talked all the time. She was always ready to reminisce—though that is a mild word for the purposive thing she did. The evocation of the past seemed more like a calling with her. The present was the projects, illiterate neighbors, a family more *incurred* than chosen, for there had been no choice. The past was where she lived and had her being. It was youth, and home. It was also full of horror. I cannot remember a time when she thought I was too young to hear those stories of war and death. But we both had been brought up on fairy tales—and what were her stories but more of the same, full of beauty and horror.

She had been a girl, like me—but how different her girlhood from mine. And I never doubted that what she was, what she had been and where she came from, were superior to me and my world. ("What you Americans call an education!" "What you Americans call an ice coffee!")

In memory I see myself always trying to get her to talk. Silence was a bad sign with her. When she was really angry she would not speak to you, not even to answer if you spoke to her. Once, she did not speak to my eldest sister for weeks.

Toward the close of a long dull day. I have lost the thread of the book I am reading. As so often on a Saturday at this hour, I don't know what to do with myself. Outside, it is getting dark. Nothing but sports on TV. My mother sits across the room, knitting. She sits on the sofa with one foot tucked under her. She is wearing her navy-blue sweater with the silver buttons, which she made herself, and which I will one day take with me, to have something of hers when I go away. (I have it still.) The soft, rhythmic click of the needles. At her feet the ball of yarn dances, wanders this way and that, looking for a kitten to play with. On her brow and upper lip, the pleats of concentration. Will it annoy her if I interrupt? (She is so easily annoyed!) I let the book close in my lap and say, "Tell me again about the time they came to take Grandpa to Dachau."

Motorheads is a word you would use today for the men of my mother's family. In half the photographs I have seen of them there is some sort of motor vehicle. My grandfather and my uncles and many of their friends were racers. In the photos they are wearing black leather jackets and helmets. Sometimes someone is holding a trophy. In one astounding photo my grandfather and five other men round a curve, a tilting pyramid, all on one motorcycle. The stories took my breath away. Motorcycle races across frozen lakes. Spectacular, multivictim accidents. Spines snapped in two, teeth knocked out to the last one, instant death. What sort of men were these? Speed-loving. Death-defying. Germans. They slalomed too.

The year I was born my grandfather opened an auto-repair shop in the Swabian town where he had lived all his life, a business later passed on to the elder of his two sons. I do not remember him from the one time I met him, when I was taken as a child to Germany. The memory of my grandmother, on the other hand, is among the most vivid I possess. "You took one look at her and called her a witch." So I already knew about witches, at two. Pictures show that she really did have the sickle profile of a witch. And I was right to fear her. She locked me in a dark closet, where I screamed so loud the neighbors came.

My grandparents had grown up together. An illegitimate child, my grandmother was adopted by the childless couple who lived next door to my grandfather's family. In summer, the narrow yard between the two houses was filled with butterflies. My grandparents were said never to have had any interest in anyone but each other, and to have shared a strong physical resemblance all their lives. My grandmother was known for her temper. During the war, when shoes were all but impossible to get and her son Karl lost one shoe of his only pair, she pummeled his head with the other; he still has the scar. Whenever my mother, the eldest child and only daughter, spoke of her mother, she tended to purse her lips. ("We were always at odds." "She didn't like girls.") When I met her for the second and last time, I was in my twenties and she had not long to live. Dying, she was still mean. A habit of reaching out and pinching you as you passed: teasing, hurtful. The pinching malice peculiar to some little old ladies. Revealing things my mother had kept from us: for example, that both of my sisters were illegitimate, and that my mother was too. ("You didn't know?") She suffered all her life from bad circulation and died of a stroke.

My grandparents were Catholics, and at that time in that town, most of the power was in the hands of the Catholic Church. Like other Catholic towns, somewhat slower to embrace National Socialism. I am not sure how much danger my grandfather thought he was courting when, just before the national election in November 1933, he stood outside the town hall distributing anti-Hitler leaflets. Before this, he had shown little interest in politics. His opposition to the Nazis grew largely under the influence of a friend named Ulli, who planned to leave for America if Hitler got more than seventy-five percent of the vote. My grandfather's two siblings were already in America, having emigrated in the twenties, but neither of my grandparents wished to leave Germany. My grandmother also may have influenced her husband against the Nazis. Her father had been an official of the Social Democratic party. She had had many leftists among the friends of her youth and had been an admirer of Rosa Luxemburg. She was arrested with her husband immediately after Hitler's victory.

"They woke us up in the middle of the night." "The Gestapo?" "No, no, just the regular town police." My mother was six. "One of the policemen was someone I knew, an old man. I used to see him in the street all the time, he was very nice. But after that night I was so scared of him. Any time I saw him after that I ran the other way."

They searched the house. Earlier that night, while my mother slept, Ulli had come to the door. "Hide these for me." A gun, a typewriter.

A policeman—"not the old one"—opened the hall closet, and the typewriter slid off the top shelf. He covered his head just in time. "I remember, his face turned bright red."

"Gerhard and I stood together on the stairs, crying. Karl slept through it all—he was just a baby."

My grandparents were led out to the waiting police van. "It was already filled with people."

"Out of nowhere" a woman appeared. "A complete stranger. She was very stern. She told us to go back to our room and not dare to come out."

The next morning my grandmother returned, alone. Later, after dark, she took the gun hidden in the wall behind the toilet and buried it in the backyard.

Eight months before, Heinrich Himmler had set up the concentration camp at Dachau. It now held about two thousand inmates. My mother said my grandfather never talked much about his time there. "He was ashamed of having done something so stupid." In one beating he suffered a broken rib that healed grotesquely—"like a doorknob on his chest." "You are going home," he was told, and put on a truck with a group of fellow prisoners who were driven to the train station. The train came and went. The prisoners watched it come and go. Then they were driven back to the camp. This happened many times. Meanwhile, there was work to be done. The camp was expanding. My grandfather was put to work installing electrical wiring. And one day, thirteen months after his arrest, he really was let go. He was sent home in his prison uniform. My mother was playing in the street when another little girl ran up, scandalized. "Christa! Your papa is coming across the field—and he's in his pajamas!"

"He was lucky." Ulli did not get out of Dachau until '45. (And then he left for America.)

My grandparents' house had been confiscated, their bank accounts closed. My grandmother had moved with the children into the house of her in-laws. She had taken a job in a drapery shop.

My grandfather was afraid that no one would hire him. He appealed to an old friend from polytechnic days, now at Daimler-Benz. A relatively quiet time began. Every day my grandfather took the half-hour train ride into Stuttgart. He was not troubled again by the Nazis. And when, after Hitler's speeches on the radio, my grandmother carried on—Hitler-like herself, according to my mother—

my grandfather said, "Let Germany follow her own course."

Time passed. The town synagogue was closed. The town idiot, a homeless man who begged on the church steps, disappeared. The main department store went out of business. The gardens of the houses where the Jews lived became overgrown. Consternation among the Mendels. They want to go to America, but Oma is stubborn. The very mention of crossing the ocean makes her weep. Finally, a compromise is reached: The Mendels will go with their little boy to America, Oma will go to Switzerland. Before leaving she entrusts two trunks to my grandparents' care. "I'll want them back someday."

Nineteen thirty-nine. My grandfather was called on a blue and sunny midsummer's day. He was with the troops that invaded Poland, and would remain in the army until Germany's defeat.

Meanwhile, my mother was growing up. Away, mostly, at a Catholic boarding school in the Bavarian Alps.

The nuns are hard. My mother comes home with a horror tale: a cat smuggled into the dorm, discovered by Sister and thrown into the furnace! Still, her parents send her back.

For many of the girls, returning year after year, from age six to eighteen, the school *is* home. Away, my mother is homesick all the time; but at home, especially over the long summer, she pines for school.

At the end of one summer, the girls arrive to find the nuns replaced by men and women in uniform. The nuns, they are told, have returned to their convent, where they belong. From now on, my mother's education is in the hands of the Nazis.

Over the next few years, many of the new teachers will be soldiers wounded in the war: amputees; a math professor whose face was so scarred, "we thought at first he was wearing a mask."

As she recalls, no one ever made any reference to her father's disgrace; she was not treated any differently from the other girls.

She keeps up her grades but she does not excel. Unlike her brothers, she is not superior in math. She does not seem to have been ambitious, to have dreamed of becoming something.

(Up to this point, I have had some trouble seeing my mother. Even with the help of photographs, it is hard for me to imagine her as a little girl. Unlike a lot of people, she did not much resemble her adult self. The child of six crying with her brother on the stairs, running away from the old policeman—I see that girl, but she could be anyone. But now, she is beginning to be familiar. I can imagine her, her feelings and her moods. I can see her more and more clearly: Christa.)

School trips to the opera. ("He who would understand National Socialism must understand Wagner"—Hitler.) Hot and stuffy in the balcony. The agony of itching woolen stockings. She would always hate opera. Today: "All I have to do is hear a bit of it and my feet start to itch like I haven't washed them for weeks!"

Another thing she hated: her turn to tend the rabbits, raised by the school for food. The filth of the cages. The fierceness of one particular buck, known to the girls as Ivan the Terrible.

The Hitler Youth. Uniforms, camping, sports. "Just like your Girl Scouts."

The rallies and the victory parades. "Tell me what kid doesn't love a parade." A little flag on a stick. Flowers for the soldiers. Always something to celebrate. April 20th: the Führer's birthday. My mother has just celebrated her tenth. He marches through the Munich streets, veering right and left with outstretched hand. His palm is warm. Photo opportunity. Later, back at school, a copy of the photo is presented to her. She bears it home, proud, *somebody*. Her mother tears it up. My mother threatens to tell.

School pictures. My mother in her winter uniform, looking, like most of the other girls, comically stout. ("We probably had three sweaters on underneath.")

Trude, Edda, Johanna, Klara—my mother's little band.

Girls becoming women. One's own tiny destiny absorbed into that of the *Volk*. To be a *Frau und Mutter* in the heroic mold, champions of the ordered cupboard and snowy diaper. The body: nothing to blush about but always to be treated with respect. My mother earns high marks in gymnastics. She is good at embroidery and crocheting.

Dance lessons. Ballroom steps, the taller girls leading.

The heart-swelling beauty of the landscape, especially at sundown. Alpenglow. Someone called it: Beethoven for the eyes.

Lights out at nine. Talking verboten. Whispers in the dark. Confessions, yearnings. Boys back home. Teachers: "I don't care that he has only one arm." Gary Cooper. The Luftwaffe aces. And: "Leni Riefenstahl was so beautiful."

In the summers, you had to work, at least part-time. You

might be a mother's helper, or work on a farm. You had to bring written proof that you had not idled your whole vacation away. As the war deepened and you got older, you were assigned labor service: delivering mail, collecting tickets on the streetcars, working in factories or offices.

The last year of the war, eight girls assigned to track enemy planes in the same operations room in Stuttgart are killed by a bomb. Among them my mother's best friend, Klara.

The last battles. Only the German victories are announced. But who cannot read the increasingly somber miens of the teachers. Letters from home tell of brothers, still in school themselves, called to fight. "Erich sends his love and asks you to pray for him."

Still, when it comes, the announcement is shocking. "You must make your way home as best you can. Don't try to carry too much with you. And be careful. There are enemy soldiers everywhere—and some of them are black."

My mother had already had a letter from her father at the front. "When the war ends, don't be foolish and try to outrun the enemy. Try if you can to hide until they have passed. Do not let them keep driving you ahead of them. It won't do you any good, they'll just catch up with you anyway. And whatever you do, do not go east."

My mother boarded a train, but long before her hometown station a roadblock appeared and the passengers were put off. Against advice she had packed all her belongings. Now she left two suitcases on the train, keeping only her knapsack; she would soon abandon that too.

(It is at this point that my mother finally comes in clearly, on this four-day walk home.)

For the first stretch she has company—other people from the train headed in the same direction. But for most of the journey she is alone. She is not afraid. Just days ago she turned eighteen. The sense of having an adventure buoys her up, at least for a time. Also, in the very extremity of the situation, a certain protection: "This can't be happening." Blessings: weather ("That was a beautiful April"), and she is in good shape from Alpine hiking.

Dashing for cover at the sound of a motor. *The enemy is everywhere.*

Hunger. She cannot remember her last good meal. At school, day after day, cabbage and potatoes. The tender early spring shoots begin to resemble succulent morsels. At dusk she knocks at a farmhouse and is given an eggnog and a place to sleep in the barn. The steamy flanks of the cows. Infinity of peace in that pungent smell, in the scrape of hoof against board. Morning. Rain. "Dear God, just let me lie here a little bit longer."

Sometimes she sings out, as people do, from loneliness, and for courage. "Don't ask me, for I'll never tell, the man I'm going to marry."

What passes through her mind cannot properly be called thought, though her mind is constantly busy, and she loses herself in herself for hours at a time. Daydreams bring amusement and solace. Her senses are lulled and she is carefree. Funny thoughts do occur to her now and then, and she laughs out loud. Sometimes she watches her feet, and the fact that they can move like that, right, left, right, covering the ground and bearing her along, strikes her as nothing less than miraculous.

Often she is light-headed. She imagines her head floating like a balloon above her. Attached by a string to her finger. She jerks the string, and her head tilts this way and that, like the head of an Indian dancer.

People met along the way move furtively, every one in a hurry. "No one would look you in the eye."

Straw in her hair, itching between collar and neck. Seams loosening with wear. The smell of the cows mingled with her own. A burning sensation in the folds of her flesh. Will she ever get to change her underwear?

She mistakes a turn, walks for miles down the wrong road before turning back. In the fields, the first wildflowers. A tumult of sparrows. She is seized by the unbearably poignant sensation of déjà vu.

A plane. Nowhere to hide. She squats where she is, arms over her head. The plane swoops down, low, so low she can make out the grinning face of the (British) pilot, who salutes before taking to the sky again. Laughing, she embraces her knees and bursts into tears. In that moment of terror her heart had flown straight to her mother. From now on she will often be struck by fear, foreseeing her house in ruins, and her mother dead.

(A young woman fixed upon reaching home and Mother, making her way through a conquered land overrun with enemy soldiers: I read that part of *Gone With the Wind* with a swell of recognition.)

At last: the church tower, the wooden bridge. A woman in the *Marktplatz*, weeping, weeping.

My mother beat the Americans by one day.

➤

The Occupation. A time to count your blessings—"at least for us it really was over"—as the refugees streamed in from East Prussia. The Americans: "You know, typical American boys—loud, friendly, vulgar. Every other word was f-u-c-k."

One day an American lieutenant came to the door. "Jewish boy, grinning from ear to ear. 'You don't remember me? I've come for the trunks my grandmother left.' We couldn't believe it. Walter Mendel, all grown up. He brought us our first Hershey bars."

Incredulity, the sense of this-isn't-really-happening, endures. A topsy-turvy time. Dating the enemy. Fräuleins in the arms of American soldiers. Eating themselves sick in the mess hall hung with Stop-VD posters: Don't Take a Chance, Keep It In Your Pants.

For my mother, the start of a new life.

(And here I begin to lose her again; I mean, I no longer see her clearly. About this period—so important to me because directly connected to my own coming into being—about this period she hardly spoke at all.)

She has a job, teaching kindergarten, which does not suit her. She doesn't particularly like children, and since these are the children of farmers, she has to keep farmers' hours, going to and coming back from work in the dark.

Whatever energy is left over goes into dating. First in her heart is Rudolf. He is her own age, a boy from the neighborhood, grown in the years she was away into stripling-handsomeness. Had her life been happy she probably would have remembered her experience of him as a lark; instead he became the love of her life, her one and only.

She said often, "I should have married him"; but just as often, "I couldn't have married him, we would never have gotten along, we were too much alike." In other ways too, she hinted at an intense and dramatic entanglement. But I don't think it really was like that. I think she convinced herself that it was, because this helped her. There is consolation in seeing oneself as a victim of love. (Ideally, of course, Rudolf should have died—killed, say, as so many other German boys his age were killed, in the last months of the war.)

"After him, I really didn't care what happened to me."

Rudolf. One precious photograph included in the family album. Curly hair and a curl to his upper lip, from a scar, giving him a somewhat cruel expression; and indeed it was by cruelty that he got that scar: He taunted a rooster, who flew in his face. He was fickle, he liked to make my mother jealous. Well, two could play at that game. From among the throng of GIs my mother picks the least likely: half-Chinese, half-Spanish, and almost as old as her parents.

Two can play the game, but for men and women the stakes are not equal.

My mother becomes pregnant.

Lacan says: Only women's lives can be tragic; about men there is always something comic.

Newsreels from this era show that the attempt to turn women who had consorted with Nazis into laughing-stocks, by shaving their heads, failed.

The next period of her life is the one I have most trouble imagining. I think it also must have been the hardest. "I thought I had died and gone to hell." But it was only Brooklyn.

The housing project looked like a prison. "Your father had said something about a house with a little garden. What a fool I was." (She often called herself a fool. Another thing she said a lot: "You made your own bed, now you have to lie in it." She had little sympathy for people who'd botched their lives, and toward real sinners she was unforgiving. She often complained that criminals in this country got off scot-free. And she was suspicious of repentance. You could not escape punishment by confession or apology. She herself rarely apologized. I'm not sure to what degree she applied her own harsh rules to herself. I know only that she suffered a lot.)

She was not the only German war bride in the projects. Now and then a group of them would go into Manhattan, to Eighty-sixth Street, to shop in the German stores. When there was a bit of extra money, a German movie; coffee and cake at the Café Wagner, or at the Café Hindenburg, said to be where the New York branch of the Nazi party had held their meetings.

I am daunted when I try to imagine her pregnant. In those days she was a slender woman, almost frail. In photographs her mouth is dark, the corners lifted, not in a true smile, but more of a my-thoughts-are-very-far-away expression. I try to picture her in one of the humiliating maternity dresses of the day ("a large bright bow at the neck or a frilly bib will draw attention away from the stomach"). She wears her long hair pinned back.

When I try to imagine her, she becomes stilled: a figure in a painting. She sits in an armchair that she has turned toward the window. From this angle you cannot tell that she is pregnant. Her one-year-old and her three-year-old lie in the next room; she has just gotten them down. She is exhausted, so heavy in her chair she thinks she will never rise again.

Blue smudge like a thumbprint under each eye. What is she looking at? Through the window: water tower against leaden sky. What is she thinking of? Schooldays. A million years ago! Trude, Edda, Johanna, Klara. Klara dead. And the rest? Surely none so unhappy as she? Rudolf! At last she bestirs herself: With a furious gesture she wipes a tear from her eye.

I don't like to remember what she told me when I was twenty: Becoming pregnant with me was the last straw.

She used to say, "If we'd had money everything would have been different." I didn't understand why we didn't get help, like many of our neighbors. "Welfare! Are you mad? Those people should be ashamed." But she was already ashamed. I saw it in her face when she had to tell people my father was a waiter. I thought taking money from the government would be better than always complaining. "You want us to be like the Feet?" (The family next door was named Foot.) "Ten kids to support and the father sits around drinking." But wasn't Mr. Foot better off than my father, who worked seven days a week and never took a vacation? Didn't happiness count for anything in our house?

There were periods when my mother cried every day. If you asked her why she was crying she would say, "I want to go home." Other times, when she'd "had it" with us, when she made it clear that we were more than any person could bear, with our noise and our mess and our laziness, she would threaten to leave us and go home. (I think I sensed something in those threats to go home that I'm now sure was there: the threat of suicide.)

About the Germans Nietzsche has said: They are of the day before yesterday and of the day after tomorrow; they have no today. Coming of age, my mother had shared in the dream of a grandiose destiny. Now she became one throbbing nerve of longing.

We believed her when she said that every night she dreamed she was back in Germany. She made us promise that when she died we would bury her in Germany. "In German soil," is what she said. She understood those Russian soldiers who had gone to war with a pouch of soil around their necks so that if they fell, a bit of Russia would be buried with them. She had the Teutonic obsession with blood and soil. She made us promise also that if she was ever in an accident, we would not authorize a transfusion. She would rather die than have someone else's blood in her.

I am seventeen, a freshman in college, invited to dinner by one of my professors. Helping his wife with the dishes, I start humming a tune. The woman looks hard at me but says nothing. Sometime later, the professor asks me whether I knew what I was singing. I tell him what I thought it was: an old German song; my mother used to hum it sometimes when she was doing her housework. He says, "Actually, it's the Horst Wessel song." The anthem of the Nazi party.

A few years before this, I had gone with my mother to a record store on Eighty-sixth Street, where she was surprised to find an album of German marching songs. "I can't believe they would sell this here." Back home, watching her listen, I saw that look of bewilderment and tenderness that comes over the faces of people when they are presented with something that recalls times past. I saw that same look on her face sometimes when we watched newsreels from the war years on TV, and though I was not there when she watched a videotape of *Triumph of the Will* (she'd been taken to see the film more than once as a schoolgirl), I'm sure she was touched in the same way.

She never played the record again. "I just wanted to hear it that once."

Now and then came packages from Germany, which often included sweets. Once, a box of small bottle-shaped chocolates wrapped in colored foil and filled with liqueur. My mother's eyes lit up. "I haven't had these for years!" But before tasting one she wavered. "I shouldn't, it will just remind me of home." A good thing she warned us: From the way she slumped in her chair we might have thought she'd been poisoned. I will never forget the sound she made. Many years later, to thank me for taking care of his plants while he spent Christmas in Denmark, a neighbor of mine brought me back a box of those same chocolate bottles, and at the mere sight of them I felt as if a poison had entered my veins.

Heimweh. "Another word you have no English for." Homesickness? "Yes, but more than that." Nostalgia? "Stronger than that."

She had a pretty voice, my mother. She sang all the time—always German songs. I liked especially "Lili Marleen." Often she sang the melody of a song, without words. Her version of the Horst Wessel song was molto adagio, more like a torch song than a call to arms. I had trouble reconciling that melancholy tune with the words when I eventually came across them in a book. "Raise high the flag! Stand rank on rank together. Storm troopers march with steady, quiet tread."

"Deutschland über Alles": "A real piece of music, not like your unsingable 'Star-Spangled Banner.'" I remember hearing something Haydn said of his "Emperor" quartet, from which the music for the German anthem was taken: In his moments of deepest despair, he would listen to it and be comforted.

Now I want to recall those words of Virginia Woolf, about childhood: "A leaf of mint brings it back . . . a cup with a blue ring." Nazi Germany was the only Germany my mother knew. Her whole youth had been lived under the sign of the swastika. She never said it, but it had to be true: When she saw the swastika, she thought of home.

In third grade I had a friend named Hannah Segal. Her mother too was from Germany. Mrs. Segal's accent was only slightly different from my mother's. "Doesn't she want to go back?" "Oh, no, she would never go back, she hates Germany." Strange!

When I was growing up, the Germans you saw in movies or on television were almost always men in uniform. They had sputtering accents and scars on their cheeks. They moved like oafs. They blundered and shrieked. They could not have struck fear in a dog. I knew better. I knew that Germans were to be taken with utmost seriousness. I knew that Germans could command so you would have to obey.

I was ten when Eichmann went on trial in Jerusalem.

My first view of the famous photographs. "Should Eichmann Be Punished for His Crimes, and If So, How?" (Essay competition.) I was twelve when I read the *Diary* of Anne Frank.

One night I dreamed I met Anne Frank in a wooded area near the projects. She was hiding out. She had escaped Bergen-Belsen and survived all these years (though she was still a young girl). She didn't want anyone to know. She would not believe me when I told her that the war had been over for years, and the Nazis no longer existed. She made me promise not to give her away.

It was said that all Germans were on trial with Eichmann. Neighbors fascinated by the testimony prodded my mother for details of life in the Reich. She never brought up her father. ("It would be as if I were making excuses.")

"I am still proud to be German." "I do not apologize for being German." But during this time she was depressed. By then we had moved away from Brooklyn, to another housing project, where there were no Germans. My mother might hang out with the other women on the benches, but she was not really friends with any of them. She would never feel at home among Americans. She had the European contempt for Americans as "big kids." She found herself constantly having to bite her tongue; for example, when one of the women complained about the war: "I don't know what it was like for youse over there, but here you couldn't even get your own brand of cigarettes."

I don't think a day went by that she did not remember that she was German. Watching the Olympics, she rooted for the Germans and pointed out that, if you counted East and West together, Germany came out ahead of both the Americans and the Russians.

It was not to be hoped that any American—let alone an American child—could grasp what this unique quality of being German was all about. I don't recall how old I was, but at some point I had to wonder: If you took that quality away from her, what would have replaced it? What sort of person might she have been? But her Germanness and her longing for Germany—her *Heimweh*—were so much a part of her she cannot be thought of without them. To try to imagine her born of other blood, on other soil, is to lose her completely: There is no Christa there.

She saw herself as someone who had been cheated in life—but cheated of what, exactly? Not a career. She never missed having a job. She was not one of those women who can say, If I hadn't had a family I'd have gone to med school. (Back then, people would say of certain women: She never married, she was a career girl.) My mother always saw herself as a housewife. During one especially lean spell, when it looked as if she might have to earn some money, the only job she could think of was cleaning houses. But just because she saw her place as in the home didn't mean she was happy there. The everlasting struggle against the soiled collar and scuff-marked floor brought on true despair. In that struggle, as every housewife knows, children are the worst enemy. Her big cleaning days were the darkest days of my childhood. She booted us out of one room after the other, her mood growing steadily meaner. We cowered in the hallway, listening to her curses and the banging of her broom, awaiting the inevitable threats to go home. Many were the objects in that house that we were not allowed to touch. We were allowed to sit only on certain chairs. When she got a new couch, loath to expose it to wear and tear, she left it wrapped in the plastic it had come in. It stayed so clean under there, she ended up wrapping the chairs in plastic too.

We offered to help her clean, but she refused. "All you do is smear the dirt around." Besides, she was not going to be one of those parents who use their kids as servants. (Mrs. Foot, for example, who had her six-year-old girl doing the vacuuming.)

Everyone had his or her proper sphere. "You kids just worry about your schoolwork."

"If we'd had money, everything would have been different." In the ads for lotto, people tell their dreams, which often turn out to be of travel, preferably to exotic places. But seeing the world was no more one of my mother's dreams than being a doctor. What would she want? A big house. A big yard. "And a big fence!" No more living on top of other people!

She would live in one housing project or another for most of her adult life.

She never played lotto. She thought chance played too large a part in people's lives as it was. And she didn't believe in good luck anyway.

I don't know that her life would have been different if she'd had more money. In later years, when my sister wanted to hire someone to clean for my mother, she refused. Maids: "They just smear the dirt around." (Dirt.

Contamination. The horror they inspired in her went deep. When she spoke of dirt encountered somewhere— someone else's house, say—she would shake herself like a drenched dog. We were not allowed to use public toilets, which made going anywhere with her an ordeal.)

Money. Visiting me in my first apartment, she happened to hear me tell my landlord that the rent would be a little late that month. She didn't understand why I wasn't ashamed of that. She had been uneasy too about my applying for a college scholarship; she would rather have paid. She would never understand how I could accept loans and gifts of money from other people. *Down to my last penny:* Why didn't I blush when I said that? "I don't know how I could have raised a daughter like that."

A simple life. Up in the morning, the first one. Fix the coffee, wake the others, bundle them out the door. Dishes, beds, dust. The youngest child home for lunch. Dishes, laundry. Sometime in the afternoon, between lunch and the children's return, a pause. Lose yourself in a book. Page 50. Page 100. An errant duke. A petty dowager. A handsome and truehearted stepbrother. The heroine swathed in shawls against castle drafts. *Romance.* A thing ludicrous to imagine with her husband, with whom she had never been in love. At best she treated him like one of the children: "Wipe your feet off before you step in this house!"

Her early heartbreak (Rudolf) had made her defiant. She didn't owe anyone anything. She didn't have to be nice. "I can't stand to be in the same room as you!" She wasn't going to play the hypocrite. "I wish that we had never met!"

A riddle: If it was true what she said, that she expected nothing from her husband, why was she forever seething with disappointment?

The threat to divorce him became part of her litany of threats. But she was never interested in anyone else, not even after he died, though she was then just forty-six. I think the idea of having an affair embarrassed her. And: "One husband was enough!" Certainly the subject of sex embarrassed her. (I come home from a pajama party burdened with new knowledge, something that, for all its preposterousness, I sense with a full heart must be true; but when I ask her whether people really *do it,* without hesitation she says no.

Wife and mother: Dissatisfying as that role may have been, it is hard to imagine her in any other. Outside the house she lost her bearings. Any negotiation beyond that required for simple domestic errands flustered her. She hated going out. She hated having to deal with strangers. Even worse: running into people she knew. But she was always cordial. She would stop and chat—often at length—putting on a chumminess that I feared others would see through, and I guess some did.

She was intimidated by authority. My decision to change my major my junior year in college bothered her. "Are you sure you don't get into trouble for that?" "You sure they let us park here?" she would ask, peering anxiously about. Some part of her always remained that child on the stairs watching the arrest of her parents. The ringing of the telephone could stop her heart. An unexpected knock at the door, and she would widen her eyes in warning at us, a finger to her lips. We all held our breath.

When the person had gone, she would peek out from behind the window shade to see who it was. Whenever she had to go somewhere she hadn't been before, she was terrified of getting lost. Her fear revealed itself in flushed cheeks and repeated swallowings; I held on to her icy hand. Oh, the trouble you could meet going into the city! Much better to stay home. At home *she* was the authority, the only one permitted to do as she pleased, to be herself.

It was as a teenager, I suppose, that I decided that maybe what she needed was the right man. In our neighborhood there were many examples of the rugged type: men with square faces and corded arms, who earned their living by brawn. I thought my mother might have been better off with one of them. (But this was my fantasy; she never expressed any attraction to such men.) Her upbringing had resulted in a paradox: Though she feared authority, she approved of it, she would have liked to see more of it. (The trouble with Americans? They are too free. The trouble with most kids? They are not disciplined enough.) Perhaps her ideal man would have been a cop. At any rate, she needed someone strong, the sort of man with whom a woman feels safe. A scoff-at-your-fears sort of man. She implied that her father had been something like this, before Dachau. My father—fumbling, shy, so fearful of authority himself—would not do. She was the one who had to drive, who carried the kids' bicycles up and down the stairs. She wore the pants. Like so much else, this whetted her scorn. "My lord and master—hah!" No sympathy for him when he was down with a cold—"He sneezes twice and it's the end of the world"—or when for a time he had nightmares and often woke her with his cries. Nor did she expect sympathy from him. Only once did I ever see her turn to him: when her father died.

Outbursts triggered by his gambling, his English, his superstition against making out a will. Once started, she could not stop herself. Her rage tore like a cyclone through the house. Afterward we would all sit in a kind of stupor in which the cat and even inanimate objects seemed to share.

My mother sobbed. "I'm not asking for that much." But she was: She was asking him to be someone else.

Finally, it was enough that he kept himself apart, letting her take care of the house and the children as she wished, leaving her alone. A large element of relief when he died: She was no longer daily *reminded.*

At times it seemed as if she had but one emotion: loathing. I think she often experienced what Rilke described: "The existence of the horrible in every atom of air."

She had that love for animals that is unmistakably against humans. "Now I know men, I prefer dogs." This remark of Frederick the Great's—quoted by Hitler—expresses a famous German sentiment. My mother: "I feel worse if I see a dog suffering than if it were a man." Said without apology; with a tinge of pride, even. As if it were superior, to prefer dogs. In one of the houses of a zoo I went to in Germany, the visitor comes to a plaque announcing the animal to be seen in the next cage: the most savage creature of all, the only one to kill its own kind, to kill for pleasure, and so on. A mirror behind bars.

When I was there someone had written in English on the wall under the plaque: "You krauts oughta know!" And under that was written in French: "Of all our maladies, the most virulent is to despise our own being—Montaigne."

But she was not without pity for humans. Once, she went into the city to do back-to-school shopping and gave all her money to an old woman begging outside A & S.

She never forgot the hunger of the war years. "Aren't you going to finish your ice cream? You'll regret it. When the war comes, there won't be any ice cream." (I worried a lot about the coming war and had my doubts whether hiding my head in the crook of my arm as we did in school shelter drills was going to save me. At any rate, when the bombs fell I wanted to be home. I knew in case of attack we were supposed to go down to the cellar, but my mother said she would never do that. She remembered raids in which people had drowned in cellars where the pipes had burst. "I rather die any way but that—drowning with the rats!" I agreed, and for a time my bad dreams composed themselves out of these elements: sirens, rats, and the water reaching to my chest, to my chin . . .) At the time of the Cuban missile crisis she went back and forth to the supermarket until the cupboards were jammed. For Easter our school held a contest in which pairs of children played catch with raw eggs. ("Only in this country do they teach children to throw food around.") They say a European housewife could feed her family on what an American housewife throws away. Suppers from my childhood: boiled eggs and spinach, knockwurst, scrambled pancakes with applesauce. My mother's love of sweets would eventually cost her every tooth in her head. Sometimes we made a whole meal out of a pie or a cake. We ate Hershey bars between slices of white bread for lunch. In our house you did not get up from the table until you had cleaned your plate. A common punishment: to be sent to bed without any supper.

I don't think I ever saw her truly relaxed. Some part of her was always going—head, hand, foot. Even when she was sitting still her breath came a little fast. I suspected that she had high blood pressure. No way to know for sure, since she never had it checked. She wanted nothing to do with doctors. Though she suffered from headaches aspirin couldn't touch, she would not go to a doctor for a stronger prescription. When small growths like blisters appeared on the whites of her eyes, she removed them herself with a sewing needle. "But you'll get an infection!" "Ach, don't be silly. I sterilized the needle." Who needs doctors?

She had good hands, and she wanted always to be using them. At Christmas she baked and decorated dozens of cookies, storing them in tins with slices of apple to keep them fresh. She copied scenes from children's books onto our T-shirts using Magic Marker, and covered her bedroom walls with a motif of abstract flowers made with crumpled paper dipped in paint. She learned to sew first of all for economy, but then an obsession took hold of her. Day after day we would come home from school to find the beds unmade, dishes in the sink, and my mother at her Singer. After a long day of sewing she would spend her evenings knitting. She made everything from bathing suits to winter coats. She was like a maiden in a fairy tale, spinning, spinning. Soon the closets bulged. All that work ruined those beautiful hands. The scissors raised a great welt on the knuckle of the third finger of her right hand, and crushed her thumbnail. Instead of being proud of her work, she would rather have had others believe the clothes were store-bought. I *was* proud, and bragged to my friends that she had made my new red corduroy coat. Liar, they sneered, when they saw the label she had sewn in the lining.

She had a green thumb. Neighbors brought her plants that seemed in danger of dying. And she saved from dying too a score of sick and injured animals—squirrels, birds, a cat that had been trapped in a burning house. I remember as blessed those times when she was engrossed in nursing some creature back to health. It was good to see all her gentleness brought out. For those hands that could make plants bloom and heal a broken wing could also destroy and cause pain. They tore things and smashed things. They pinched, slapped, and shoved.

I sit on her bed watching her get ready to go out. The process of putting on her face takes a long time and is always the same, but I never tire of it. Those tempting little pots and tubes with names like desserts: Iced Mocha, Plum Passion, Peaches 'n' Cream. The magic mascara wand. Abracadabra: blond lashes are black. She says it helps if you keep your mouth open when putting on eye makeup. She is in her slip and stockings, the bumps of her garters standing out on her thighs. When she crosses her legs, there is the hiss of nylon against nylon. She says that

European women are better at using cosmetics than American women. "American women look so cheap." She always puts her lipstick on last, but first she rubs a dry toothbrush lightly across her lips to smooth them. I pick up the tissue she uses to blot her mouth and fit my own mouth to the imprint. The next part of her toilette I don't like. Before pulling on her dress, to protect it from stains, she ties a scarf over her face. Standing there in her nylons and slip with the scarf over her face she is a disconcerting sight.

People said, "Your mother is so pretty." But she didn't see herself like that. I could tell by the way she spoke of other women that she did not count herself among the pretty ones. She was not flirtatious. She was never charming in a strictly feminine way. She had no use for feminine wiles, and she hated being ogled by men. She would not wear clothing that drew attention to her figure. Her daughters were another story: "When you are young you can get away with anything." Not all agreed. The dean of boys stopped me in the hall. "Does your mother know you're walking around like that?" "She made this for me." "Well, tell her this is a high school, not a skating rink." I was chagrined, but my mother laughed. "It's his own guilty conscience that's bothering him."

She didn't like to go to parties where she might be asked to dance. "I don't want a strange man putting his arms around me."

She never complained about getting older. She looked much younger than she was. Once, on her way to the store, she crossed in front of a police car and the patrolman called out through his bullhorn: "Young lady, shouldn't you be in school?" "I gave him a dirty look and kept walking." I knew that look. I'd seen her shoot it at a lot of men. In time her coldness toward men would seem to me a miscalculation: Hadn't she ever considered the possibility that being nice to men could get a woman things she might not otherwise have?

Though she would always color her hair she gave up trying to stay slim. As she put on weight, her jaunty walk became more of a waddle. You would not have thought she had once been good at gymnastics. But she could still bend from the waist with straight knees and touch her palms to the floor.

She might not enjoy going to parties, but she threw herself wholeheartedly into helping me get ready for one. She made my dress. She did my hair. She got into a competitive spirit: "You'll be the prettiest one there." By the time I was in high school her moods in general tended to be brighter. I think it had to do with her children growing up. I was the only one still at home. Young enough to be still under her thumb but old enough not to be a burden. I did well in school, I made her proud. (But if someone complimented me in my presence she would shake her head. "Please. She thinks highly enough of herself as it is.") She was curious about all aspects of my life and took pleasure in those adolescent triumphs: making cheerleaders, being asked to the prom. The carefree, promising youth she herself had not known.

(I spent the summer of my twentieth year in California. One day my friends and I took acid and went to the beach. At sundown, driving home in our jeep, we were still high.

On acid, every passing thought can strike like an epiphany, and this one seemed to fill my head with light: My mother had never known this. To be driving with your friends in an open car, laughing; to be twenty and happy and free with the wind in your hair and your life ahead of you—she had missed all that.)

My friends liked her. She was different from other mothers; prettier, livelier, more fun. She enjoyed making people laugh. She would have you on the floor, doing toothless Rufus who ran the corner store, and his half-wit wife. Her dislike of men never extended to the boyfriends her daughters brought home. She was often at her best when one of them was around. She cooked special dinners and knitted sweaters for them too. I had boyfriends who, years after I'd stopped seeing them and moved away, would still call her from time to time to say hello. She took it hard sometimes when I announced that she wouldn't be seeing a certain boy at the house again. I suppose she too could have wanted a son.

She was no liberal, but something about the sixties appealed to her. The antics of the Yippies, bra-burnings, the way the hippies got themselves up—she got a kick out of all that. She liked to see a bit of spunk now and then. You could light up a joint right in front of her. "Now just a minute," she'd protest, but she was only playing her part. My friends thought she was cool. She was pleased and excited that I went to Woodstock.

I found her everywhere in my reading. Children are said to see images of their own mothers in the stepmothers and witches of fairy tales, but I always saw mine in the innocent blond girl, often the prisoner of the witch, forced to labor at her sweeping or spinning. Later, I would identify her with any damsel in distress, with romantic heroines like Anna Karenina, Emma Bovary, and Scarlett O'Hara.

I placed her under the sign of beauty, suffering, and loss.

Sitting on her lap as she pages through a magazine. One ad after another showing beautiful women in beautiful dress. "You should wear this, Mommy." "You would look nice in that." Her response is gruff. "And where would I wear such a thing—to the laundry room?"

The hours and hours she spent beading the gown I would wear to the country club dance.

She swiftly disabused us of certain notions acquired at school. America is the land of equal opportunity. All men are brothers. The best things in life are free.

Home for lunch, I eat my sandwich while she sits at the kitchen table, pasting S & H Green Stamps into a book.

The hum of her sewing machine. The funny munching sound of her pinking shears. "'My Lili of the lamplight . . .'"

Sometimes I would catch her looking at me with a gently stricken expression. In a sad voice she would say, "You are a good kid, you really are."

Her favorite English poet was Tennyson.

She said, "Give women power and they'll turn out to be worse than men." (She always expected the worst of people. She thought humankind was irredeemable. Her punishments were always given more in anger than in sorrow.)

She had strong opinions about everything. Opinions should be strong, otherwise they are not worth having (Goethe).

Her people, the Swabians: known for their bluntness and for their love of order.

She was different. She did not *belong*.

"How in God's name did I get here?" she would ask, her head in her hands, truly bewildered; as if she had blown here like a feather.

When I was in grade school I remember she used to write poems based on themes from mythology. She made the costumes for some of our school plays. Always a supply of pink and blue yarn (in our neighborhood someone was always having a baby).
No one I ever knew had such smart hands.

At her lowest she would say, "I feel like a bug crushed under someone's heel."

I believe that, in spite of all her railing against her lot, she never really expected anything different.

You made your own bed, now you have to lie in it.

I don't believe my mother made her own bed.

➤

Often, when I said that my mother was German, people wanted to know: "*How* German?"

Her accent: described by one friend of mine as "so German it makes your skin crawl." The accent of the mad doctor. "Und now, zee injection." The accent of the murderer, the torturer. "Vee haf vays of making you talk."

After her mother died, in the early seventies, my mother went to Germany and brought back some mementos, including a box of photographs. Most of the people in these photos were strangers to me. A chubby, smiling boy of about ten: Albrecht, 1918. A cousin of my mother's mother. "He grew up to be so handsome, you never saw anything like it. How can I describe him? You know Hitler's master race? Well, he was the ideal: blond, blue-eyed—and in his SS uniform he was a god. He rose very high in the SS. Ach, don't look at me like that. He was in the Waffen-SS, he had nothing to do with the camps. He was a good, decent man. What? Who knows. After the war we never heard from him again. Not even his wife knew where he escaped to. South America, probably."

When I was growing up, whenever I threw a tantrum she would say, "Who do you think you are, a little Hitler?"

I must have been about seven or eight when Mr. Blum first came to the house. Mr. Blum was from Berlin. He had escaped to America in the thirties, when he was in his teens. Now he worked for the welfare department. He and my mother met in our building one day when she was downstairs getting the mail. ("He took one look at me and started speaking in German.") After that he dropped by sometimes when his work brought him to the projects, though I gathered such visits were against regulations.

He wore a black patch over one eye, like Godfather Drosselmeyer. He had a large head with damp-looking wavy gray hair, and large hands with fingers so long and thin and pale they made me think of candles. He looked ancient to me (it was more that patch than the gray hair.) In fact, he was probably about ten years older than my mother.

The morning they met at the mailboxes was a Saturday and I was home. My mother had been gone so long I started to worry and went downstairs to look for her. When he saw me Mr. Blum turned to my mother and said, "You married a Japanese?"

The next time I saw him was in our living room. "What happened to your eye?" "The cat ate it." "I don't believe you." "You are right, my dear, I am lying. I tell you what really happened. One day, you see, this eye got very tired. I took it out to give it a rest. I put it in my pocket for safe-keeping, and when I went to get it again, it was gone!"

I liked Mr. Blum. I liked his peculiar tweedling voice. His voice was a rocking horse, rocking, rocking. My mother pretended to be merely putting up with him—"I thought he would never leave!"—but that's not how it seemed. They had so much to talk about. They talked for hours at a time, half in English, half in German, fortifying themselves with two pots of coffee and a dozen pastries between them. They talked about people in the projects, including Mr. Blum's cases, and we children were warned not to repeat what we heard. Of course, even when it was in English much of that talk was cryptic to me. ("And it turns out the father of the baby is the father of the mother.") Sometimes they talked about the war. (Mr. Blum had fought in France.) They talked about before the war, and I noticed that often—usually—instead of saying *Germany* they said *Europe*. For example, speaking of any number of things you could get "in Europe" and could not get here: good bread, good butter, a decent education.

I knew that Mr. Blum lived about a half-hour's drive from us, and that he too had a family, including a son at NYU—"a real beatnik, that one." That we were never invited to his house and never met any of his family did not seem to me odd; Mr. Blum never met my father either.

Now I can't recall whether they always argued, or whether this was something that developed only after a time; I do seem to remember many visits ending in a quarrel. Mr. Blum was a terrible tease. He would say to my mother when she opened the door, "I come to see your half-Aryan *Kinder!*" He hardly ever called her Christa, but rather Greta, Gretel, Gretchen, Heidi, Ilse, and so on, in his teasing way. He baffled me. "Why do you call my mother Greta?" "For Greta Garbo, of course. Because Garbo's face is the ideal to which your mother's face aspires." He made me cry one day when he said, "You are nothing but a little monkeyface compared to your mother."

He said also, *"Deine Mutter ist meshuggah."* And once, when he was talking about a house he had been to, I thought I heard him say, "In every naked granny was some little trot-sky."

I remember how my mother's eyes blazed when he said that violence ran in every German's veins. But then immediately he added, "I am teasing, Heidi. You know how I love to see you get mad." But sometimes, hours after he'd gone, she would still be fuming. "Why does he come here? He just wants to insult me. Next time, I throw him out. Bastard. I don't know why I even let him in."

Once, she did not let him in. She knew that he was in the neighborhood, because she'd seen his car parked in the lot behind our building. She sat on the couch with her arms crossed high on her chest when he came to the door. Seeing the look of satisfaction deepening on her face as he knocked and knocked, as if he knew we were there, I felt as great a fear of my mother as I have ever known.

And then came the big fight, the one that ended with her demanding that he leave and not come back. Though it was in German, and though I was in my room and missed most of it, I could have told you what it was all about. It would have begun with one of Mr. Blum's jabs, wounding my mother in her *Deutschtum.* She would have tried at first to hide her feelings, not wanting to let on how much he had gotten to her. He would have persisted, probing at the chink in her armor. In the explosion that followed, Negroes, Indians, and Hiroshima would proba-bly all have been dragged in. My mother would have accused somebody—or everybody—of being a hypocrite and holier-than-thoo.

When I arrived on the scene, my mother had just said something at which Mr. Blum made a noise like water in a slow drain and waggled a finger at his eye patch. Later it would occur to me that what he said next was probably something like "I saw it with my own eyes." But at that moment I took him to mean something else.

As he was gathering up his hat and coat, I slipped out of the house and down the stairs, and that is where he found me moments later, by the mailboxes, where we had first met. I had told myself that if I really was never going to see Mr. Blum again I must say goodbye. But as he stood looking down at me, hands on hips and head cocked expectantly, a more urgent need of mine found voice. "Was it the Nazis who poked out your eye?"

Mr. Blum made a little popping sound with his breath, followed by a word I didn't catch and which probably wasn't in English anyway. By then, however, the horror of what I'd just done had sunk in, and I would have bolted back up the stairs had not Mr. Blum started to speak. "If I remember correctly, when I was your age it seemed to me everything in the world was created to give the maximum confusion to my brain. What can I say? It won't always be like that. You will grow up and go places, meet people, do a lot of things. Go to college, even. Read books. The Bible and Shakespeare and maybe even a little bit Freud. And the world will look completely different to you from what you know here in the projects. Because here you don't get a clear picture of life at all, believe me. Anyway, your mother says she doesn't want to see me again, so——" (Why did everyone always do what she said?) He extended his long pale fingers, and when I touched them I was not surprised to find that they were as smooth as wax. He dug a handkerchief out of his pocket. Earlier, I'd seen him blow his nose heartily into that handkerchief, but I didn't mind that he now used it to dab my face.

In fact, that was not the last time I saw him. He and my mother made up. His visits continued, and so did the fights. And then he changed jobs, or he moved, or something, and he stopped coming to the house. I don't remember any last big fight. I don't remember anyone missing him. From time to time his name would come up and my mother would shake her head and arch her brows as if to say, What a character! And soon we all forgot him. I grew up. I went to college. Read books. Shakespeare and the Bible and a little Freud. Why did he come? Why did she let him in? What happened to his eye?

Another memory, from several years later.

It was the winter of the mohair sweaters. My mother had already knitted quite a few of them for me, in different colors. I wore them to school to the envy of my friends. "Your mother is unreal." (But one teacher disapproved. "What are you afraid will happen to you if you wear the same outfit twice?") The sweater my mother was working on now was a tender shade of blue. We were watching a movie on television: *A Place in the Sun.* My mother told me that the book on which the movie was based was called *An American Tragedy.*

This was at a time in my life when I had just begun to worship Elizabeth Taylor. I thought that she and Marilyn Monroe divided the world between them, with no third. I had little sympathy for the weakling played by Montgomery Clift. I did not even find him very handsome. Though he was the one whose life was at stake, it was the Taylor schoolgirl I was concerned about. The story was of the sort calculated to feed certain notions that had recently possessed me. It seemed to me that in most cases (as in *A Place in the Sun*), a man who suffered a tragic fate had had at least some part in bringing it about; in some cases, had even deliberately gone in search of it. Whereas women—especially beautiful women—could expect to have tragedy thrust upon them. In those days Elizabeth Taylor made the papers at least once a week. Like the typical victim of an infatuation, I imagined that I understood her in some special way. No matter what record-breaking fee she was getting for *Cleopatra,* I knew that she was not happy. It was common knowledge that she was susceptible to respiratory trouble, that she was not supposed to let herself get run down. Once, she almost died of pneumonia. The divorces, the rumors about drinking and pills. You had to worry. Look what happened to Marilyn Monroe.

I adored romantic movies, above all for the women, many of whom I placed with my mother under the sign of beauty, suffering, and loss. I wanted my mother to watch these movies because I thought she could learn something from them, as I hoped I was learning, about how a woman ought to be. As I say, I thought her coldness toward men was a mistake. I saw the way men looked at her and it made my heart pound. I'm not talking about the leers, though there were plenty of them. I'm talking about a look that was gentle and melancholy and urgent, and that helped me to understand what he meant when years later I came across Valéry's words: The ardor aroused in men by the beauty of women can only be satisfied by God. At that time in my life I could not imagine any future happiness that did not depend on a man, and I lived for the moment of that transfiguring embrace at which all fear and uncertainty would fall away from me. Anxiously, I studied the mirror. Although many people said they thought my mother and I looked alike, just as many said they saw almost no resemblance. And hadn't my mother herself said that men wouldn't look at her twice if she were a brunette?

At the end of *A Place in the Sun*, after a last visit from the priest, Montgomery Clift is led away to be executed. We are shown what is on his mind—the image he will carry out of the world with him fills up the screen: the face of Elizabeth Taylor.

I sit back in my chair, sated with the sorrow and the beauty of it all. But when I turn to my mother I see that she is buying none of it. She holds the length of blue yarn up to the light and shrugs. "God. What you Americans call a tragedy."

She got old, she became a grandmother, but she didn't look like a grandmother, and she wasn't grandmotherly. Her moods continued to be better than they had been when I was growing up. She was not so often depressed; even the migraines ebbed. But she began to have other troubles. Dizzy spells, shortness of breath. Once, in line at the supermarket, and a second time, at home, she fainted. But she would not see a doctor. She got in the habit of saying, "You'll never get me to a hospital," and "I want to die at home."

She did go to the hospital once, long ago, to have a cyst

removed from her neck. It was a hard time for us children, who weren't sure what was happening, and who, being under twelve, were not allowed to visit on the wards. She came home with a thick white bandage taped across her throat. It bothered me a lot, that bandage. It bothered me even more when it came off a week or so later, revealing that sinister scarlet smile. The idea of the vulnerability of the throat—the image of a throat laid bare to a knife— became fixed in my mind. (Elizabeth Taylor's famous tracheotomy most likely played some part in this.) I would never be able to wear chokers or turtlenecks or anything that fit snugly around the neck.

I never saw her at a loss for words. She was always able to say what she wanted to say. She always knew how to say what she was feeling. Her memory was excellent, as were her powers of observation. Nothing escaped her, you could not put anything over on her. I think she had a good mind.

But as a mother her instincts were often wrong. My first day of kindergarten she knew I was afraid and might give her trouble. She led me into the school building and showed me the door I was supposed to go through. I looked where she pointed, and when I turned around again, she was gone.

She so believed in the efficacy of corporal punishment that she was baffled when it failed. "Poor Mrs. Reece. No matter how much she beats that son of hers he still steals."

Although she insisted that you obey all the rules without question, she was disdainful when you asked to do something because everyone else was doing it. "What are you, a sheep?"

She had no best friend, no one—besides her daughters, as we grew older—to whom she could really talk, no confidant. She didn't trust people. If anyone tried to get close to her, she backed away. "People are too much trouble."

And yet, people trusted her. People poured out their hearts to her, even some that she hardly knew. People told her things that they said they had never told anyone else. She was a good listener. While the other person recited the story of his or her life, she would not interrupt or allow her attention to wander. Her head wagged from side to side or up and down understandingly. As a child, I would listen in on these talks, no less attentive. But with the years I lost my tolerance. I discovered that, with people who insist on telling you the story of their life, usually it's a sad story. I hadn't my mother's infinite capacity to hear such stories. Nor did my mother forget what she'd heard once the person was out of her sight. The stories took hold of her, and she in turn insisted on repeating them. In later years, when I'd come to visit her and she'd start in—about the mailman, say, whose son had stolen from his own mother's purse even as she lay dying of cancer—I would cut her off.

It was the same with the animals. Young, I was delighted to come home from school and find that we were once again giving shelter to some helpless dog or cat. But in time I grew to dread the unmistakable smell that would hit you as soon as you opened the front door. Many of these animals were in bad shape. Many had been abused, in some cases by people we knew. My mother didn't believe in doctors for animals either. She doctored them herself, using a book she'd found in a secondhand shop. Not all of those animals survived.

When she finally moved from the projects into her own house, she fed packs of strays from her back porch. In bitter weather she built shelters of plastic and cardboard in the yard: an animal shantytown. She fed the birds and the squirrels too.

Twenty years passed between her first and her second trip back to Germany. After that second trip she returned a number of times. But she never moved back. After all those years of pining for home—why not? "Because it isn't home anymore. Remember: The Germany I knew is gone. The Allies bombed it away. There is hardly anything of the Old World anymore, everything is new. And it's just like everywhere else now, Germany. Changing all the time, getting more like America every day. There are tourists and foreigners everywhere you go. The cities are crowded and noisy and polluted. The Rhine is dying. The Black Forest is dying. And most of the people I knew there have either left or are dead. Why would I go back now?"

I want to ask her whether she still wants us to bury her in Germany, but I refrain.

Back in Germany that first time, she realized that she was forgetting her German. "I go into a store, I want to ask for something, and for a second I have to struggle for the German word." With the years she lost more and more of her German, and at some point—she doesn't remember when—she began thinking in English. After living in America twice as long as she lived in Germany, she finds that German has become her second tongue. She stops reading in German. Dining in a German restaurant, she orders in English. But her accent remains as thick as it ever was, and she still makes the same mistakes. "They stood in a motel for a week."

(She was not the only one in her family to become an American. Soon after she arrived in Brooklyn, her youngest brother, Karl, not yet out of his teens, came to stay. Drafted into the army, he did part of his training in North Carolina, and lost every trace of his German accent; an impeccable Southern drawl replaced it. Under that hot sun he grew in quite another direction from his sister. He saw himself as an American through and through. He never left the army. On his second tour of duty in Vietnam he married an eighteen-year-old Vietnamese girl who was already expecting their second son. My uncle brought her and their first son to the States. One night he suggested that he and she and my mother and father go out together. It was the year of *Bob & Carol & Ted & Alice.* My mother said, "You know what people are going to think, don't you?")

Twenty years passed between my own first and second visits to Germany. The second trip took place soon after I graduated from college. By that time already it had become a fad: digging up one's roots, traveling to the land of one's parents, describing how it felt to set foot for the first time on the soil trod by generations of forebears. That tingling of the blood, sense of homecoming, and always, and perhaps most important, pride. Imagine feeling that way about Germany.

I met Germans, young Germans, who had been born in or after Year Zero. On being German, every one of them agreed: It's a drag. On the New Germany: It is boring. Jokes about impenitent old Nazis gathered in the day rooms of nursing homes, watching *Triumph of the Will* over and over again. The young people were all saving their money to go somewhere else. Paris, Rome, San Francisco, New York. I would see some of them again when they came to live in New York.

In the tourist publicity, the words used most often to lure visitors to Germany are *romantic* and *fairy tale.*

I was in the Old Pinakothek in Munich when it occurred to me: Germany was like an Old Master that had been given too many cleanings.

But what had any of this to do with my childhood?

People who remembered said, "When your mother brought you here that time, the children called to one another up and down the street, 'Come and see the children from China!' We got a kick out of that."

But we didn't look that Chinese.

"Well—compared to them."

Taunted in the schoolyard once when I was a child, I went to the teacher who was on recess duty. "Those boys are calling me a half-breed." The teacher said, "Well, you aren't one, are you?" I paused, uncertain. Uncertainly, I shook my head. "Well, then, it shouldn't bother you."

The last thing I would have believed back then was that one day it would be fashionable to be Chinese; or that I had only to wait a few years, till I reached adolescence, to hear people say that they envied me my exotic background.

Myths.

Being of mixed race makes you immune to many diseases.

Women of mixed race are uncommonly lustful.

A famous conductor, introducing a half-black, half-Jewish pianist to a concert audience, suggests that the pianist's talent is a result of his being mixed.

In college, at the beginning of every semester I received an invitation to join the Asian-American Student Society. A Chinese-American man I met much later said, "I got those in school too. That's what I hate about the Chinese: so damn clannish. You can't be yourself, you have to be one of them." He admonishes his brother, who arrives to lunch wearing a short-sleeved white polyester shirt and dark polyester slacks: "Do you have to dress so damn chinky?"

Another time, at a party, a different Chinese-American friend asks me to play Ping-Pong. I have never played before and I tell him I don't know how. He says, "Don't be silly, of course you do: It's in the genes."

Genes. Blood. Soil. Why should I feel a deeper pain on hearing that the Black Forest is dying than on hearing about the dying forests of the Adirondacks? And what is this surge of feeling inspired by a photograph in a magazine: a group of smiling Asian-American children: *Those Asian Whiz Kids!* Pride?

Memory of another teacher, on her knees, hugging me and pleading, "Promise me you'll never forget that you're just as good as any other little American."

When I talked about my mother and father people often said things like, "Only in America." People called their story "a real American story."

The apartment in the projects had a kitchen, a living room, a bathroom, and three bedrooms. The linoleum on the kitchen floor buckled here, curled up there. The windows were the kind you have to crank open, and they had mustard-colored shades that were replaced by the housing authority every three years, though long before that they would have torn or lost their spring. Winter. My mother lays a hand against the radiator. "Freezing!" She pulls her navy-blue sweater tighter around her. "If I don't get out of here soon, I lose my mind!"

For a time when I was very young I used to wind my hair around the fingers of my right hand and tug. I did this mostly in my sleep. When a small bald patch showed on the back of my head, my mother made me wear one of her nylon stockings as a nightcap to bed.

At that early age I often dreamed that I was being crushed by some—Thing. A living, heavy-breathing Thing, covering my entire body, bearing down, crushing, smothering. Murdering.

Older, I had many dreams about trying—and invariably failing—to rescue someone. It might be a child in a burning house, or someone about to fall off a roof or get hit by a car. These dreams persisted into adulthood. In a foreign, war-stricken land—jungle or bush country—I come upon a group of starving natives. I sign to them that I am going to get food, and that they should wait for me. I go and come back, lugging a big steaming pot. But in my absence the enemy would have come and slaughtered them all.

One morning an old woman who lived alone on the top floor of the building across from ours was found lying dead on the ground. Because she was clutching a rag in one hand, some people thought she must have fallen while trying to wash her windows. Later, one of the maintenance men reported that they had found nothing in that woman's apartment when they went to clean it out except a mattress on the floor and a single spoon.

What is a home? In the ten years after I left my parents' house I lived at fourteen different addresses. This constant moving taught me not to accumulate or to set too much store by possessions. (Yet I am someone who is incapable of traveling light; I want to take everything with me. Traveling in general causes extreme anxiety in me.) I have never had much success at establishing a proper domestic life. (Home economics: the only high-school course I truly hated.) For years I ate off paper plates. I don't cook. I can't sew. If there is a leak I stick a pan under it and leave it there. ("I don't know how I could have raised a daughter like that.")

But I am always happy in a nice house. I am in awe of those who know how to make things homey. Comfortable chairs in rooms with sun, flowers in a vase, clean sheets, home cooking—no one could be more appreciative of such comforts than I.

The trouble I have traveling goes beyond the shyness and vulnerability felt by most people when taken out of their familiar world. What I feel is something closer to bereavement. This feeling is associated with the memory of two fictional scenes that have haunted me since childhood, one from a book, the other from a movie. Which book, which movie, I cannot now say, but both scenes are set somewhere in Europe, in train stations, during wartime.

In the scene from the book, a man puts a little girl—his daughter—on a train. He is sending her off to safety somewhere. Father and daughter wave to each other as the train leaves the station. The man watches the train until it is out of sight: "And in his heart he knew that he would never see her again."

In the movie, which I saw on television, a man is seeing a woman off. He is wearing a soldier's uniform and he is on crutches—he has only one leg. The man and the woman wave to each other as the train leaves the station. As the train picks up speed, the man hobbles along the platform, faster and faster, until he stumbles and falls.

Since that trip to Germany I have been back to Europe, but not to Germany. I have never been to China.

So not everyone lives as if a sword were hanging over his or her head! The discovery came with growing up, with going out into the world and meeting people to whom no harm had ever come and who lived, to my endless astonishment, as if no harm would ever come. I didn't know what to make of such types (I am thinking now mainly of people I met once I got to college). They seemed to me to be lacking something, which I often mistakenly thought was intelligence. Many of them came from reasonably happy, prosperous families and from a kind of order that my mother, for all her passion for order, could never achieve. Over my childhood hangs the memory of perpetual violence: quarrels, fits, punishments. Threats and curses rang through those years. It was imperative to escape.

Once, struck by a slamming door, I lost consciousness briefly, and when I came to I saw something I was sure I hadn't seen before: the face of maternal anxiety. In that moment I remember surprise and joy at this undeniable proof that she cared.

Long after that first day of kindergarten, I would still think about it. I never could figure out how my mother managed to disappear so fast when my head was turned. It was as if she had vanished into thin air.

Fear of impurities, love of obedience, preference of animals to men. Like my father, my mother also seemed at times bent on conforming to stereotype. She got a dog, a Doberman pinscher, and she named him Woden.

It was on one of her visits back to Germany that she learned that Rudolf, who would have turned sixty that year, had died of a heart attack. She reported this months later, in passing, with a simple shake of her head. It was no big thing to her.

When my mother and my father appeared together in public, which was very seldom, people stared.

No wedding photographs in the family albums.

But this: from the same box that contained the picture of my grandmother's cousin Albrecht, a picture of my parents, taken just before they left Germany for America. A candid shot, catching both of them with their mouths open. They have linked arms and they are leaning into each other, as if for support—so hard are they laughing. Arm in arm, laughing. No, I would never have imagined my parents like that. But even more incredible: One of my sisters insists that she remembers a time when she came upon them kissing and kissing. (Of course one's memories of one's early life are not reliable. It is possible that I have got innumerable things wrong. It is not impossible that one day I will have to write my parents' story all over again.)

That sister would in time find herself trying to persuade my mother to get a divorce. The marriage had been a mistake—who could deny it? No one was happy—why let it go on? My sister believed that my mother owed herself another chance; it was not too late for her to find happiness with someone else. My mother said that even though she wanted to she could not leave my father; she said her conscience would always bother

her if she did. As for someone else, again: "One husband was enough!"

Secretly, I imagined that she had lovers.

She could laugh at herself. She often did laugh at herself—sometimes even through tears. Wiping her face with the back of her hand, crying, calling herself a fool, laughing, making jokes about her own stupidity.

One wants a way of looking back without anger or bitterness or shame.

Resemblances between her face and mine became more obvious with the years. I have her voice and her handwriting.

Sometimes, when I am tired, say, or upset, or drunk, I may start to speak with a slight accent. My first year in college an English professor asked, "Why does your writing read like something translated from the European?"

I don't believe there is much Chang in me.

That first day of kindergarten, after she vanished, I did not go through the door that my mother had pointed out to me. I just stood there in the hall, breathless, trembling, staring at the door, until at last it opened and a pretty young black woman who would find a place in my heart forever as Miss Lord appeared. Smiling, bending forward from the waist, holding out both hands to me.

Now that I recall, in those dreams, it was always a woman or a child needing to be rescued, never a man.

There are times when I seem to remember my mother as though she were a landscape rather than a person. Those blue eyes filled the entire sky of my childhood.

I think I know what *Heimweh* means.

It was Nietzsche's idea that when one has not had a good father one must create one. But of course he was thinking only about men.

Time and again I discover that I have not completely let go of the notion that salvation will come to me in the form of a man.

Once, when I was driving with my mother, another car skidded and came hurtling toward us, missing us by a hair. At the moment when it looked as if we would die, she said, "Mama."

What is love? In yoga, there is an exercise in which you close your eyes and try to imagine a bright white shining light, then to think of someone and to send that light to him or her and imagine it pouring down, surrounding and protecting that person. I have never been able to do this exercise without my eyes filling with tears.

One wants a way of looking back without anger or bitterness or shame. One wants to be able to tell everything without blaming or apologizing.

Message on my answering machine: *Mom fainted again today. Please call.*

Freud says the most important event in a man's life is the death of his father.

Oh, Mother.

A
FEATHER
ON THE
BREATH
OF GOD

The dream of being a ballerina begins with the dream of being beautiful.

It wasn't my mother who decided I should take lessons. I made that decision myself, swept away not by any performance but by a series of photographs in *Look* magazine. I was almost twelve then. Much time would be wasted later wondering what my life might have been had I come upon those photographs sooner.

I have not been inside a ballet studio for many years. Going back, I am led by that most powerful organ of memory, the nose. Sweat, rosin, and Jean Naté, the freshener many dancers used to splash on after class. The sweat-soaked wooden floors had their own pungent odor. The beloved reek of the studio. For me, a holy smell, signifying work, sacrifice, and ardor. (I have been in classes full of people sweating hard at aerobics, but the sweat of ballet must be different; it is not the same smell at all.) It was in the studio that I learned for the first time that some people work out of love. Dancers were paid pennies in those days, but you never heard anyone complain; you never heard the word *money* at all.

I had never met anyone who had taken ballet and I didn't know what to expect. Because of my age I was placed in a class not with raw beginners but with girls who had been studying for about a year. I was told to watch one particular tall blond girl and to follow her; if I was "clever" I'd be allowed to stay. That girl was a natural who later became a principal dancer of the company. Years after my feet had stopped, my heart was still following her.

Our teacher was a Kirovian fury. Down the years I can hear her. That voice: If you could have held it in your hand, you could have cut glass with it. Oh, Madame could cut. I don't think she had more than fifty words of English, but it was enough. To drive home a point she would turn in her toes, stick out her rear, and loll her tongue. "Like this you are looking. Yes! Is you. Pretty, eh?"

The accent, the cuttingness, the mimicry: Whom did she remind me of? But she was old enough to be my grandmother.

That first day, I gripped the barre to keep from fainting with fear. But I went home from that class on air. Everything about the world of ballet responds to the young girl looking to escape real life. An aura of other-worldliness about dancers like that of nuns. Those who are drawn to ballet are looking for order and discipline. The struggling ballerina believes in perfection. And to see a fine dancer execute a pure arabesque is to believe that the body, at least, is capable of perfection.

Balance, symmetry, motion, shape—in a word: art—it was all there, that first day in the studio. The classic posi-tions of ballet seemed to me as beautiful as anything in nature. Not that I had seen much of nature. Up to then, I had not seen much of anything outside the projects. But one thing I could say for sure about ballet: It was at the opposite end of the world from the projects.

Black leotard, pink tights, pink shoes—no other clothing allowed. Ribbons worn round the ankles, knees, or waist must also be pink. Hair must be kept long and worn up for class. Hairpins must hold. (Pretty but unwelcome sight: the whirling dancer's hair flying out from her head.) No lateness, no talking, no sitting, no leaning, no slouching, no gum-chewing. If your feet hurt, if you were exhausted, you were unwise to show it. I loved it all—the rules, the rituals, the intolerance of any slackness or leniency. Authoritarianism was, of course, in keeping with my upbringing; but now all the rules had a purpose. Ballet meant finally being taken seriously; meant being allowed to take yourself seriously. It gave me back some of the dignity that I felt was constantly being undermined elsewhere in my life. The tough public schools I went to were famous for discipline problems. In ballet class no one was ever disobedient or disrespectful. At the end of every class came the reverence: Each girl made a curtsy to the teacher. This custom struck me as weird and even a little ridiculous the first time I saw it, but I came to cherish it as I did everything else about ballet.

In class, everything was straightforward. As usual my mother was right. There was only one way to do anything, and that way was never easy. There were these steps; you were told which ones to do and how and when, and you did them. Everything was as clear and as inflexible as glass. In spite of the pain and the tedium ("Repetition," say the

Russians, "is the mother of learning," and class meant repeating the same exercises until it hurt to do them), I was never bored. I might be disappointed in myself, in my own lack of talent or progress, but ballet itself could not possibly disappoint.

Work as hard as you can. Make it beautiful. How can you argue with rules as pure and as simple as that?

I once read an interview with a musician who said he considered himself one of the luckiest men alive. "Imagine that it's your job to play Mozart!" I never met a dancer who didn't feel that dancing was its own reward. Nothing else in my life would ever live up to it.

I don't believe there was a single day that I did not look forward to class. Changing my clothes in the cramped, shabby dressing room (it may be different now, but back then the study of that most gorgeous of arts apparently could be undertaken only in drafty old buildings, amid bad plumbing and peeling walls), I would suffer the needles of anxiety: Every class was like a little performance. But once at the barre, with the first plié, everything fell into place. For the next hour and a half I would know who I was and what I was doing and why, and that was not at all the way I felt most of the time. I would be *fully present*, as I rarely was outside of class. It was a new and empowering feeling. On good days there were moments when I felt as if I were dancing in a shaft of light.

But above all else, ballet meant escape. Instead of going home after school, I could go to class. In class, concentrating on my tendus, I could forget all about my hopeless parents. And there was the excitement of traveling into the city, which I loved, and which I promised myself would one day be my permanent home (about this, at least, I would turn out to be right). Now, of course, I can say precisely what it was that was happening to me: I had discovered the miraculous possibility that art holds out to us: to be a part of the world and to be removed from the world at the same time.

Commuting into the city on my own made me feel grown-up and important, and I was sharply aware that my carriage, my turned-out walk, and my pinned-up hair attracted attention. "Are you a dancer?" To my joy, people would ask me that. Once, at a *Swan Lake* matinee, a woman sitting in the row behind me asked for my autograph, "just in case you make it." I would never have admitted how much this pleased me, for we students disdained, or thought we were supposed to disdain, those drooling outsiders, balletomanes. I think in fact we were afraid of them. Balletomanes tend to be critical, their hates are as strong as their loves, and at intermission, listen: You're as likely to hear them tearing a dancer down as praising her. ("God, Giselle must be getting her *period* tonight.") It was hard to hear people who had never danced (and who never would, and who never ever could) criticize any dancer's performance. In other ways too, balletomanes struck us as perverse. That unmistakable whiff of lust you got off them. In those days I would not allow that there was any erotic aspect to ballet, and I was offended whenever I heard anyone use the word *sexy* to describe it. (Even today I can't help cringing when I see *sexy* in a ballet review.) I knew, of course, that there was a world of men and women out there who were turned on by dancers. But to my mind ballerinas were chaste; it was gross to pant after them.

Of course, most people I knew in those days were neither turned on nor turned off by ballet. Dance had not yet become a popular spectacle, and although everyone knew a little girl or two who'd gone to the local dance school, it was not common for a teenager to be studying ballet. Only dancers and athletes and a few oddballs exercised passionately. If you went to Capezio, all the shoppers you saw there would be dancers. Ordinary people had no use for leotards and tights. Back then, I don't think any dancer dressing for class would have believed that one day her leg warmers would be the latest thing in street clothes, worn by women of every size and shape.

That was another important thing about ballet: It was a woman's world. A world where women not only outnumbered but bested the men. It was not just a question of feminine grace and flexibility. Women were better dancers period. And it was not just for adagio. Women could execute smaller movements faster and with greater precision than men too. The only thing men could do better than women was jump a little higher. So here was that rare thing: reason to be grateful to have been born female. It seemed to me that male dancers must often have wished they had been born female, though I never heard any of them say this. But if ballet dancing was your passion, how could it be otherwise? Men ran the school, men ran the company, men did the choreography—men called the shots, as they always do. But who cared? Men didn't get to go on point. And what is ballet without point?

It took me almost two hours to get home from dance class. The only time I had to do my homework was on the subway and bus. On weekdays, I was usually home twelve hours after I had left the house in the morning. (Saturday was the best day of the week, because I could take two or three classes. Sunday—no classes—was a waste; I was always miserable on Sundays.) I would have a quick, wordless meal with my father, wash out one of my only two pairs of tights, and go to bed. During this time I felt a great distance from my family, even more so than I would when I went away to college. I withdrew from school life as well. My grades went down, but I didn't care. I wished I could go to Professional Children's School, like some of my ballet classmates.

"If I had a dime for every time you get on that scale . . . " (My mother.)

We owe the greatest ballets ever made to one man's obsession with Woman. For him, the ballerina was ultra-woman, the feminine ideal. That her body should be one long curveless line, fleshless, all muscle and bone—a body, let it be said, more boy than woman—was one of the crazy and crazy-making paradoxes of ballet.

"You have to get to the point where the very thought of eating makes you gag a little." It is the tall blond star of our class who is speaking. "You can train yourself, you can talk yourself into it," she says, patting the sunken space under her ribs.

Advice from another sylph: "When you see food and you feel tempted, focus on what the food will turn into once you do eat it. Really think about it. It will help kill your appetite."

Strange, that none of this seemed strange to me at the time. What could have been more in keeping with that stern, pure life than fasting? And I was not much of an eater even before I discovered dance. I didn't have any sense of the pleasure food can give until I was in my twenties. In our house, eating past necessity was discouraged. My mother always complained that we ate too much. I was dazzled when I visited the houses of friends and saw how much food was kept on hand, and how casual everyone seemed to be about it. In our house you were not allowed to take food, not even a glass of milk, without asking first. My mother knew every bite I ate. And so a certain amount of guilt about eating had already been instilled in me. Now I had found my own reason to starve myself, and I had plenty of lovely company. "Americans eat like pigs," my mother said. Not me, not me.

Give a dancer a choice between a small plate of chicken and broccoli and rice for dinner, or one large brownie, and she'll probably take the brownie. Most dancers are addicted to sweets, and there were periods when I practically lived on them. Sugar was great: It could give you the zip you needed to get through a hard class, but you had to be careful. Too much could make you dizzy, and you might finish your pirouettes on the floor.

It is only to be expected that the ballerina, that female extreme, should suffer from female anxieties, pushed to extremes. The anxiety of never being thin enough, of never being beautiful enough, of being rejected after one has reached a certain age——and that age so young! It was something you saw all the time: hardworking dancers fired because someone——because some man——had decided they were too old or too fat.

And something else you saw all the time: a gifted child

betrayed by puberty. When a girl comes to audition for a school, she is carefully checked out. Is her back flexible? Does she have long legs? A long neck? What they should really check out is the mother who brought her to the audition. I remember Pamela, a very good dancer and my friend, whose doting dumpling of a mom always accompanied her to class. Years later, long after I had given up ballet, I saw Pam's mother having dinner with a man in a crowded restaurant that was known for its barbecue. I was tempted to go over to her and ask whether Pam was still dancing. But of course it was Pam herself I was looking at, and I didn't have to ask.

All the beauty magazines, which I was now reading from cover to cover, warned that the way I ate would ruin my looks. But I had inherited my father's indestructible teeth, and there was nothing wrong with my skin or my hair. This was youth, of course. But I wonder. It is said that vigorous exercise can counter all kinds of physical abuse, and that may be why so many dancers I knew appeared to be glowing with health, though they lived on cigarettes, black coffee, and Tab.

Those days when you had managed to eat nothing but one apple and maybe a candy bar, you went to bed nauseated and with a splitting headache, but also with a sense of triumph. (In dance, pain was often inseparable from desirable feelings. For years after I quit I remembered certain pains—hot, cramped, throbbing toes, for example—and I missed them. I would have forgone many pleasures to feel the pain of being a dancer again.)

Even now, outweighing my young self by almost forty pounds, when I look at photographs from that time, I don't see myself as thin. I was never thin. Not even at ninety pounds. To see how long I could go without solid food (up to five days) was a favorite game. How beautiful the hollowed gut, the jutting bones. To be light as a feather, light as a soul—"a feather on the breath of God" (Saint Hildegard).

Not all the sensations caused by hunger are unpleasant. Some days I bore a universe of stars inside my head. It never occurred to me that what I was doing was bad for me, nor do I recall anyone ever suggesting that it was bad. Masochism, anorexia—these were words I heard only much later. It could have been worse. I never ate myself sick, never forced myself to throw up, never took Ex-Lax or the popular "natural" equivalent: a box of dried apricots and tea. I knew dancers who did all these things. But during those years the seed of illness was planted. The sense that eating was a disgusting habit and that food was impure would come back to haunt me. Ahead lay periods when I would have trouble keeping food down, when I would not be able even to brush my teeth without gagging, and when, hard though I tried, I could not stop myself from imagining what the food I loathed to eat "turned into."

My best friend in class was a very thin and very rich girl named Portia. Rich in itself, that name—not any ordinary girl's name, it seemed to me, but a name for the stage. To go on stage was not just a dream with her but a kind of birthright. Her family had been in the theater for generations. She had famous grandparents. Her father had been an actor and was now a producer. Her mother had been a dancer and was now an actress. They knew a lot of dancers and actors. They knew Mr. and Mrs. Stravinsky.

We often went to Portia's on Saturdays after class. The apartment, on Park, in the Seventies, had as many rooms as a large house—an architectural possibility that had not yet occurred to me. The kitchen above all impressed me, with its pantry the size of my future freshman dorm room. As always, I was struck by the amount of food. Pyramids of cans, a whole shelf of cereal boxes; many kinds of coffee, many kinds of tea. "What would you like to drink?" The first time Portia asked me this I said, "What do you have?" She gave me a puzzled look, then laughed and said, "Anything you want, silly." And it was so.

Once again, going back in time, I am led by the nose. The whole apartment smelled delicious: bosky, summery, alpine. Never the smell of cooking that I can recall, though much good cooking was done there. It was a Chinese woman—silent as a tree, with a face in which, like a doll's, only the eyes seemed capable of motion—who cooked for the family. A woman I will never forget Portia describing as having been *lent* by her mother (along with the duck press) to a friend one evening for a special dinner party. It was that word *lent*, possibly, that fixed my decision not to tell Portia about my father. But then one day Portia's mother asked me whether I was part Oriental.

"Mommy, how did you know?" Portia was delighted.

"Oh, an old trick. If you want to know if a man is Jewish, they say, try to picture him in a yarmulke. Well, I just popped your little friend into a kimono!"

Later, as we sat in the kitchen having tea, Portia announced to the cook, "My friend is part Chinese too."

At which that woman, chopping vegetables at incredible speed with what looked like a small axe, did not even glance up.

I liked being at Portia's. It was surprisingly easy to feel at home there, grand though it was. It was very different from television. On television, when the idea was to give an impression of wealth, what you got was mostly pallor and shine. A woman with pale blond hair wearing a white gown and a white fur stole. Rooms with white carpets and white furniture, everything looking brand-new, airy, and weightless—sugar-spun, like the cotton candy my father bought me at Coney Island. But Portia's house was all darkness and pattern and heft: woodwork, tapestry, lots of heavy dark furniture. And: "It's very old," she would say, of practically everything I asked her about there.

"My parents are party animals." It was the first time I had ever heard that expression and I laughed, envisioning a scene from a children's book. I knew Portia's parents went out almost every night, and often when we arrived at the apartment half a dozen guests would already be there. "Aren't they darling?" Portia's mother would say as we entered the living room. "Aren't they two little jewels?" I had never heard anyone talk like that. But the ways of these people were all new to me. I had never seen people touch so much, I had never heard people so loud. They all talked as if to be heard in the next room, they boomed and they pealed when they laughed, and they laughed a lot, and Portia's mother often cried. Her tears were completely different from my mother's tears. "My mother is very emotional," Portia explained, in the same tone she might use to say, "My mother is out shopping." A striking woman, thin and supple as a willow wand, with ivory skin and large dark shining eyes, like black olives. Portia's father, years older than his wife (and only now as I picture him do I see that his stiff wavy hair is not real) liked to play the piano for his guests, songs I would not identify until later as those of Cole Porter and Rodgers and Hart. Sometimes people would sing along, and sometimes Portia's mother would say, "No, not that one, please, or I'll cry." But her husband played the song anyway, and she did cry, but instead of being angry when he finished, she kissed him.

So much kissing. Women kissing women: That too was new to me. I tried to imagine the women of the projects embracing each other, calling each other darling, sitting on the benches as these women sat on the several couches that the living room was big enough to hold, with their arms about each other's necks. Fixed in my mind is a pair of dancers, sipping from the same glass, puffing on the same cigarette, and pecking at each other. The women all had names like Lili and Margot and Colette—and that is where I would meet them again: in Colette.

My mother listened with full attention when I described Portia's world to her. But she laughed her most scornful laugh when I said I too wanted to live like that when I grew up. Portia never met my parents, never visited my house. Once, when it got to be late, her father sent me home by limousine, all the way to the projects. The driver had to use a map because I had no idea how to direct him. Later, I looked for signs of a change in feeling toward me on the part of Portia or her parents and was relieved to find none. Not having any way to get Portia back to Manhattan was my excuse for never inviting her to my house.

Portia went to Professional Children's School, and as if there were not enough already to envy about her, she hardly had to do any schoolwork at all. A pretty girl, with an open, cheerful temperament. A good kid, as we used to say. She had her mother's large dark shining eyes. Confidence was the big feature of her personality. She was not that good in class. She was not as good as Pamela, she could not touch our tall blond star, and though she worked hard in class, no one mistook her for one of the destined ones. But about her future there was no doubt. It was just a matter of time. A niche was being carved for her, and one day, when the right time had come, her strong-armed father would sweep her up and set her there.

She died at the age of sixteen of leukemia. By the time I learned of this she would have been twenty-five, and I had not thought about her in years. Now I never remember her without also remembering the old Irish doorman who used to be on duty in her building on Saturdays. Pink, sunburned-looking skin and a pouf of crisp white hair, like snow on eaves. He was another one who called everyone darling. He holds the big door wide for us as we enter the lobby. Beaming at Portia, he wants to know how the dancin' is comin' 'long, and he listens as she replies, with a look all tenderness and pride, as if she were his own grand-daughter. He smiles after us as we cross the lobby and get into the elevator; he waits until the elevator door has closed, never taking his eyes off Portia. At the last second, just before the door closes on us, the light in his face goes out and his expression turns wistful, as if he were afraid she might never descend again.

The old building where the dance studio used to be was pulled down in the early seventies. Not long ago, a violent crime occurred in front of the building that replaced it. The blood of the victim has not yet faded completely from the sidewalk. The blood of a young woman.

Back then, there was no security guard in the lobby, and people came and went freely. The elevator, a large rickety cage, was at the back of the lobby, up a flight of three steps. One day, as I entered the building, a man came in behind me. We waited for the elevator together, and when it arrived we both got in. He was a young man, but his slouch and pinched features made him look older. He kept his hands in his pockets and his eyes on the floor. The elevator door was just closing when a voice cried out to us to wait, and I pressed the button to open the door again. Three young women, all going the same place as I, crowded in. And now the man got out, as if he'd changed his mind, and we went up without him.

I did not give this man another thought until the following day when I heard that he had waited there in the lobby for another few minutes, until another young dancer arrived, a girl who got in the elevator as innocently as had I and whom he forced up to the roof and raped.

That girl was not in my class and I barely knew her. No one made much of the incident, it shocks me now to recall, though she never returned to the school. But to be honest, I felt less for that girl than I did for myself. By this time in my life, I had already developed my sense of being in constant peril. I was always afraid that something was going to happen to me. (I was one child of the Cold War years who didn't need shelter drills to be convinced that the world might blow up at any minute.) I know people who would have seen such a narrow escape, had it happened to them, as proof that someone was watching over them. But I was used to feeling, whenever I heard about trouble striking someone else, how easily it could have been me. I lived under threat of harm at every moment of my life, violence and trouble were always looking for me, and if they missed me it was only by a hair, and next time they would not miss me.

Was it this incident that prompted my rash decision to change schools? At the time I thought there were sound reasons for change. I was often in pain. This almost surely had to do with my late start and the fact that I had to rush to get on point after only one year of classes rather than two or three. I would say now that I was probably suffering from tendinitis (though some of the pain I felt was bone-deep). But at that time I was not looking for a diagnosis. Pain was good; pain was promising. Pain meant that you were working hard, doing things right; it was when you didn't feel pain that you had to start worrying. Any dancer could tell you that. But I was dancing badly—nervously, gingerly, with that fear of falling that is fatal to the dancer—and I thought changing schools might help. Auditioning for the new school, I was crafty enough to lie about my age. I was hoping for a scholarship. My mother, who had expected that I would outgrow ballet and start thinking about college, was beginning to chafe about all these dance classes. A scholarship could change everything; it would take my future out of her hands.

But before he handed over that scholarship, the director of the school told me, I had to hand over proof of my age.

I don't know whether this was school policy or whether he was suspicious of me, but that was the end of that.

I know now that I had no future as a professional dancer. I never made up for that late start, never came close to really mastering even the most basic steps. Once I stopped dancing every day, I immediately lost what proficiency I had, which would not have happened to a better dancer. Nevertheless, it amazes me how easily I gave up my dream. (But then, hadn't my entire upbringing conditioned me to expect disappointment, to see futility in every effort? I have sometimes thought that I am less afraid of failure than other people because I know it is inevitable.)

I have spoken of the pain of dancing. Now let me say something about the pain of not dancing. You stop dancing and your body tightens. You feel like a piece of clothing that has shrunk in the wash. A sensation worse than any muscle ache. You are trapped in a body that is too small for you; you want to claw your way out. Was it really possible that ordinary people went about feeling this way all the time? I knew I couldn't do it. And so I danced when I was in college. I took classes in modern dance and in jazz, but these styles never much appealed to me and I was not good at them. It was only much later, in yoga, that I came close to the bodily feelings I had never stopped missing. Sustaining a balance and being stretched to the limit satisfy very deep cravings in me.

It was a long time before I tried to take ballet again, and when I did I realized my mistake and stopped immediately. It was a long time too before I could watch ballet again, and when I did I was astonished to think I could ever have been so blind. Nothing to do with sex, did I say? Hoisted into the air by her partner, the ballerina is borne down-stage, her legs split as wide as they can go, the rushing air driving her chiffon skirt up to her waist. If she is wearing a tutu, the effect is even more startling: a frilly target board with her crotch for bull's-eye.

There were times, sitting in the dark of the New York State Theater, when it seemed to me that ballet was about nothing *but* sex.

I cannot be the first to make the connection between the toe shoe and a penis—or, to be more accurate, between the toe shoe and an erection. I can remember rid-ing back and forth to class on the subway, reaching often into my dance bag to fondle my shoes, and what pleasure it was to feel them, the smooth satin, the hard points. I can remember also the special feeling, the excitement and the sense of triumph that came from développé, the slow extension of the leg out from the hip, strong and straight, foot aimed at the ceiling—the higher the leg the better the feeling.

Sitting in the audience, watching those stiletto girls with their phallic feet, I felt as if scales were falling from my eyes.

I cannot be the first to make the connection between toe shoes and foot-binding. I think a lot of people would be surprised if they knew what a dancer goes through with her toe shoes. I think some people might even find their plea-sure in watching ballet a little diminished. It takes a long time, a lot of scraped-off skin and blood, before the neces-sary calluses form, and by then the dancer's foot has become something hideous. Balletomanes who gush over a dancer's feet are talking about *slippered* feet, of course. (The

Chinese woman's bound foot—that stump incredibly called the lily—was always covered with a white sock.)

Toe shoes. Pink satin torture chambers. No left, no right—no contouring to accommodate the foot's natural shape. Pink satin slipper: favorite of the fetishists. (It fits, the rumor that Balanchine loved the huge bunions that deform every ballerina's feet.) Ballet a woman's world? But it was men who invented ballet—and the ballerina. It is men who put her feet in those shoes, and who take the food out of her mouth. All this to get the desired creature, more boy than woman, a kind of third sex—could it really be?—a woman with a penis, a woman capable of an erection.

Ballerina: beautiful, passive, mute. *Doomed.* The most poetical subject in the world, said Poe, is the death of a beautiful woman. He would have loved *Serenade.* Balletomanes use the word *goddess*—but what creature is more closely linked with powerlessness and mortality? Slave girl is more like it. (There was a time when the line between dancer and concubine was a thin one. The odalisques of art history were often ballerinas.) If the demands made on her body are outrageous, even sadistic, know that she wants it. For she is a woman who craves discipline and a master. (Said the sultan-choreographer of his favorite: "No matter what I asked her to do, she never said no.") You can do whatever you like to her. Tie her in knots, cut out her tongue, starve her, break her feet, her heart. *Of course* her life is short. Her great enemy is the enemy of all beauty: time. That tall blond girl I used to imitate in class and who had gone on to become a star: I had followed her career and knew her history of injuries and other troubles. She was forced to retire at thirty-four. I would still give years of my life to have stood on her points.

Nineteen seventy-one. Marching down Broadway. *Stop the War.* All along the route people come to their windows to watch. I look up and see at one large window a bouquet of pretty, small round heads: We had interrupted a class. The girls' faces are curious, mystified. All at once they vanish—pouf! Madame, no doubt, calling them back to the barre. The envy I felt then—and it was serious envy—was not just because they were dancing and I was not. What I envied more was that they didn't have to concern themselves with the war. They had achieved that great goal of mine: the escape from real life. There was only one thing they had to think about. (When I first heard that there existed a book called *Purity of Heart Is To Will One Thing,* I thought it had to be about this: singleness of mind, of passion, of purpose; one love, one reason for being.) I have admired but never envied people who are good at many things. I have always wanted to do only one thing well.

As a dancer, for a brief time it was possible for me to believe that the world was a simple place, bare and clear as geometry. Balance, symmetry, motion, shape. Purity of heart. Will. *Work as hard as you can. Make it beautiful.*

But why don't men go on point?

And why does the woman in *Serenade* have to die?

I knew a musician who went to medical school. In training, during surgery rotation, assisting through long operations, he would play the music he loved best over and over in his head—entire symphonies and concertos beginning to end: his invisible Walkman, he called it. I still have trouble concentrating on any work for a long time without going off and doing variations in my head.

Six-thirty on a winter evening, and I am on my way home from class. A very good class, it must have been—a class in which I must have been praised, or in which I finally got some step I thought I would never get. I peel off my wet tights, fold them into a towel, and stuff them into my dance bag. My hair I leave up, soaking wet as it is. My body is still warm and a little trembly from the big-jump combination. Out into the cold. During class, it had begun to snow. A sheet of white flannel on the ground, muffling footsteps, muffling traffic. I walk to the subway, delighting in the snow kisses that cool my flushed cheeks. Every pore of my skin has been sweated open, every cell tingles, I am aglow. A crowd has gathered outside Carnegie Hall. Two men coming from the other direction stop talking to each other and stare after me as I pass. A moment of complete magic; a sudden sense of weightlessness, of the world pulling back; the conviction that some great and wonderful thing was coming toward me. It was all I could do not to stretch out my hands.

Whatever that great and wonderful thing was, it didn't come. But the memory of that radiant moment stayed with me, melted into my skin with the snow—and returned with full force some years later, on another gentle snowy night.

End of the semester. It is very late and I am alone in my room. A narrow desk by the window, overlooking the courtyard that is slowly filling up with snow. Books open on the desk, bright lamp, cigarettes, a boyfriend's photograph. I will sit there all through the night, I will smoke all the cigarettes, and in the morning I will cross the court-yard to answer questions about literature and the tragic sense of life. The sound of a pen scratching in the night is a holy sound. I want to get down something T. S. Eliot said: Human beings are capable of passions that human experience can never live up to.

IMMIGRANT LOVE

It seems to me that the room was full of smoke, or smoky light. Or maybe it's the curtains I am remembering. It was summer—that I know. The windows were open, and there were thin curtains—pale but not very clean—slowly shifting in front of the windows, like smoke. Late afternoon of a very warm day. A house somewhere in a neighborhood I didn't know, a house I was driven to and would not have been able to find my way back to. Damp and dark as a cellar when we entered. Who lives here? I do not know. A poor home, shabby, but not wretched. The bed I slipped into moments ago was unmade. My clothes lie on a chair. (For some reason it was important to me to take them off by myself.) There is a big tree outside the window and it is full of birds, singing my disgrace, a song these birds will teach to their young and to other birds, around the world, so that now no matter where I am, in other rooms, in other beds, I sometimes wake to hear them, singing my disgrace.

The man is in the bathroom. I hear the sound of water running, a throat being cleared.

A breeze. Moving curtains. Birds.

He comes into the room and sees me lying in the bed. He unbuttons his shirt as he crosses the floor. His chest is white but his face and hands are brown. Blue eyes. Teeth. Big teeth, one eyetooth pointing out a little: sharp. Carnivore. Gold chain. Tattoo. Strong. He bends over me smiling, he opens his mouth wide, he covers my mouth with his mouth, my whole mouth. Is he going to swallow me?

Wild heart. Birds.

When he pulls back he is no longer smiling. He is looking the way he looked earlier, in the car, when he was driving us here and thought he had made a wrong turn. As he draws the sheet away from my body, I fight the impulse to curl up.

He says, "You're just a kid, aren't you?"

Sometimes, when you look back at your younger self, you feel as if you are looking not at yourself, but at another person, and that other person still exists somewhere. For many months now I have been living with the image of this girl, thinking about her, not as if she had grown up and become who I am now myself, but as if she were still to be found, just as she was, in that very bed, in that house that she could not have found her way back to.

If I could find my way to that house, I would ask her many questions: What is she doing there? Why did she go with this man? What was she looking for? Mostly I want to know how she of all people—she who is afraid of everything—is not afraid to do this.

An afternoon in June many years later. A brightly lit office in midtown Manhattan. Interview. How long have you been teaching English? What foreign languages do you know? What foreign countries have you visited? Have you ever lived abroad? Do you think you would become home-sick, living abroad for two whole years?

The interviewer, a young- and earnest-looking man in his forties, watches my face carefully. The face I choose to show him is young, earnest, a little wonderstruck, unknow-ing. It is the face he wants to see, the face that will get me this job.

There is an application to fill out. Please use black or blue ink and write clearly. I am shown into another room where other interviewees are sitting at a long table, writing clearly in black or blue ink. A map of the world on the wall. All the same questions I just answered, now asked for in writing. I wish it were permitted to smoke.

On the way home from the interview, I stop and buy some peonies. Later that day I look up from my book and I feel a pang. For they have overbloomed, as peonies do. They have turned themselves practically inside out. All it means is a sooner death for them. There seems to me something almost generous about this. *Straining beauty.* The phrase sticks in my head.

The girl is lying in bed with the man. The man is fast asleep. The girl is not asleep. She is wide awake, she could not be more wide awake, in her whole life she has never been so awake. This is no time to ask her questions. She has to get up, she has to get dressed, she has to get out of there.

Birds. Smoke.

Don't make me say how old I was.

Many times the girl has been told: If a man looks at you, do not look back. Just ignore him. Pretend he's not there.

Her father does not look at her. Her father does not know one daughter from another. But the world is full of fathers, and she can't be invisible to all of them. She cannot remember a time when the temptation did not exist for her. She was forever looking back. Her eyes grew huge with looking back.

As in all things, the girl's mother plays a prominent part. Set on distinguishing *her* child from the "icky little brats" of the projects, she dresses the girl like a dream of a little girl: white tights, short flared skirts with wide starched sashes. Even later, because the mother is the family dress-maker, the girl has little to say about what she wears. Much of what the mother chooses for her is attention-getting, revealing. The daughter quails. "I can't wear that to school!" The mother pooh-poohs her. ("When you are young, you can get away with anything.") Only much later does it occur to the girl to wonder whether her mother would have taken the same risks herself.

Do everything you can to get men to look at you, and when they do, pretend they don't exist. Because only a slut looks back. Is that perfectly clear? Early lesson on the female condition.

Very young, still a child, the girl discovers that she is drawn to men in a way that other children are not. Whatever else there might be in their attention to her, there is also kindness—she is sure she is not mistaken in this. "I wish you were *my* little girl." Reasonable, innocent desire. She is aware of delighting in her ability to make men smile. In general, she prefers the company of adults (women too, but especially men) to that of children. Adults are more appreciative, they are better listeners, and she has so much to say. Men like to touch, to take you on their knees and stroke you as if you were a kitten. She has watched kittens. Roll onto your back, turn up your stomach, tilt your head. As her eyes grew huge, now her face grows more triangular. She knows that there is something off, something unmentionable, that she cannot fathom. Over the whole picture, a wash of sadness. Again, it will occur to her only later: A lot of the men who paid so much attention to her were losers. But from those early days she takes the notion of a masculine love that was kind, furtive, melancholy. Hopeless.

Compared with her father other men are usually bigger, hairier. The neighborhood men are tough, hotheads ever ready with their fists. Some have done time. Often the smell of whiskey on them. Deep rough voices when they speak softly, large rough hands when they caress—this gets to the quick of her. A certain kind of story has a hold on her imagination during this time—the kind of story in which a child is befriended by a wild beast. A movie about a little girl and a lion. The lion is gentle only with the child; no grown-up can get anywhere near him. Another movie, seen many times on television and much loved, about a girl and a gorilla named Joe, supernaturally big and strong. Monstrous when riled, capable of immense destruction, but again, ever gentle with the girl. At the climax of the movie, he rescues children from a burning orphanage. "Joe! Joe! Help, Joe!"

(This is how it was born, I think. This is the root of that dream: He will be loving and tender. He will be strong, fierce, and brute enough to protect me from the world.)

The wish to please, to charm—the desire to provoke desire—runs deep in me and seems to have been there from the beginning. Where I learned how to flirt is a mystery to me. Certainly not from my mother, and not from my sisters, who do not share this trait with me. It was there from the beginning: more a compulsion than a trait. And the conviction—or fantasy—that I could please men, that I knew what men wanted, was always there too.

If a girl is too easy, men will not want her. I was grateful to learn early that this was a lie. But it is hard for a girl, always having to live with the threat of *slut* over her head. And *cocktease.* It was flung at me but it wasn't really true. I almost never withheld.

I do not think it can be possible that I never dreamed of marriage. But if I did, that dream died early and left no trace. What stayed with me was a horror of marriage, and I don't owe this to my parents alone. I saw no happy marriages when I was growing up—at least, not outside of television. (Once, when I complained to my mother about our family life, she shook her head and said, "You've been watching too much television.") The peaceless households of the projects. Wives and husbands forever at each other's throats, and children overwhelmed. Maybe they could fool themselves but they couldn't fool the kids: Mom and Dad wanted to kill each other. I still get anxious when I am around couples. Almost always that tension, the little digs and huffs. A woman who survives being pushed onto the subway tracks by a man from behind says, "The first thing that flashed through my mind was that it was my husband. We'd had a fight that morning."

In high school, a young woman named Miss Perce taught our all-girls' hygiene class. When she showed off her engagement ring, one of the girls asked her how it felt to be getting married. Miss Perce said, "Everything will be different now, and I know I'll have to change. I mean, I won't ever spend five dollars on a lipstick again." Maybe she said more. In fact, she must have said more. But all I remember is that bit about the lipstick and what an odd and disheartening remark it seemed. Twenty-four of the twenty-five girls in that class, I'd bet my ring finger, went on to marry. I often remember Miss Perce when I am buying a lipstick. A good one costs about twenty dollars now.

A big, cheerful family round a well-laid table. A roomy, well-kept house. A dog. A yard. Again, this dream must have been mine too, once upon a time, but it was soon replaced.

A single room. A chair, a table, a bed. Windows on a garden. Music. Books. A cat to teach me how to be alone with dignity. A room where men might come and go but never stay. I began dreaming of this room when I was still in my teens. I saw it waiting for me at the end of a long wavering corridor.

It is not just the heart that has its reasons. Surely in some language of the world there exists a word that means "for reasons of the body." The body: Nothing makes you more aware of it—of its beauty and of its ideal ability to express feeling—than dance. And nothing ennobles the body like ballet. Ballet is all about opening up (turnout: the opening of the crotch and thighs), and the great ballerina roles are full of dancing that is about the opening up, not just of the body, but of the entire being, to love. Go to the ballet, watch Giselle, watch Odette and Juliet and Aurora, and see. The wish to be all body, the dream of a language of movement, pure in a way that speech ("the foe of mystery"—Mann) can never be pure—I would not have been the same lover if I had not danced. And it has been a real ambition of mine, thwarting other ambitions, coming between me and all other goals: to be a woman in love. In love lies the possibility not only of fulfillment but of adventure and risk, and for once I was not afraid—either to suffer or to make suffer. In more than one language the words for *love* and *suffering* are the same, and I have flung myself from cliffs, I have hurled myself at men's hearts like a javelin.

But what will you do when you are old? A woman starts hearing this when she is nowhere near old. In the wink of an eye you go from slut to spinster. But was it so terrible to be an old maid? I saw myself traveling in foreign cities. Bright sun, ancient stones, the endless noon of the streets and the eternal dusk of the churches. Straw hat, sandals, a white blouse, and a skirt flaring gracefully below the knee. Dinner alone: bread, cheese, fruit. Long train rides, rocking, dreaming. *No one knows me.* The unfamiliar peace of a hotel room. The narrow bed with its iron bedstead. Faded wallpaper, original paintings touching in their crudeness. No one knows you, you can make yourself up anew every day. This evening you have written two letters and finished the guidebook. You take a long bath, and when the stranger comes, you make love on the narrow bed, no English, speak with the body. And afterward the bed is too small, good night, my dear, never forget, goodbye, good-bye.

Are there really women like this or only women who write stories about women like this?

Someone has said: To be a woman is always to be hiding something.

A woman, a wife, a mother, sits in a café with me and talks about the man she calls the love of her life. Out of her life now, this love, as he must be, for he was wrong for her in all ways but one. When she left him for good she took one of his shirts, she wanted to have something with his smell in it. It was his smell, she says, that drove her beyond reason, drove her to risk everything that was most important to her. "I keep it in a plastic bag in the bottom drawer of my dresser, and from time to time when I cannot resist I take it out and I bury my face in it."

During the time that I want to tell about now, I had a job teaching English to immigrants. (Broken English: Sometimes I think it is my fate.) Immigrants. Refugees. ("You look like a refugee," my mother used to say, whenever I was not dressed to her liking.)

The students came from all over the world, and it was another teacher who once observed that, in most of their cultures, women who lived as we mostly young and single teachers did would be considered whores. Administrative warnings about provocative clothing and friendly behavior that might be misinterpreted by some of the men.

Just arrived in America, the students speak little or no English, but class is conducted entirely in English. "Another language, another soul." A pretty saying, but not everybody is going to see it this way. The slowness of my class's progress fills me with anxiety. Oh, the stubborn resistance of the adult mind. For every one like my mother there are ten like my father, those who will never know English as a second language.

In the back of the class, by the window, sits the Russian. No better than the others at first, but soon my best student. A seaman from Odessa, but not Ukrainian, and not Jewish, as are most of the other Russian immigrants here. In fact, Vadim would never have left Odessa, he says, were it not for his wife, who is Jewish, and most of whose relatives were already in New York. He is fiercely proud of his Russian blood. The Communists may have destroyed his country, he says, but the Russians will always be a good people. ("Russians have a wide soul.")

Taller than everyone else in class by at least a head. Sharp cheekbones, slanted blue eyes, full lips, large teeth, and a way of smiling that makes you understand why we say to *flash* a smile, because that is just what he does. I think it is the smile that makes me think of a gypsy. (And what makes Vadim smile like that, apropos of nothing, in the middle of class? I find out later, what he had promised himself: "By end this class, I fuck this teacher." And every time he remembered this resolution, he would flash those teeth.)

Teaching the conditional, I ask the students to say what each of us would be if he or she were an animal. I am told that I would be a Siamese cat. And Vadim? "A wolf! A wolf!"

Nothing about him that is not long—long face, long arms and legs, long waist. In youth, a competitive swimmer; at thirty-seven, still long and lithe. An adolescent body, all muscle and bone. But the face is worn, already old, the face of a longtime substance abuser. And the hair is mostly gray. He has the throaty bass voice common to Russian men, and he wears the international uniform: black leather jacket and very tight jeans—the uniform that would not be complete without the knife in one of the pockets. (Walking in the park with him at dusk, I tense at every man who approaches. "You don't have to be afraid," he says. "I am from Odessa. I very good with knife.") When the weather turns warm, I catch a glimpse of the crucifix he wears on a chain around his neck and wonder: What must his wife think of that? In the streets of Brighton Beach, it draws stares and occasional comment. A habit of kissing it when he wants you to believe something he says: not at all convincing.

I am proud (unduly, maybe) of his progress in English—as if he could not have learned so well from any other teacher but me. At a certain point, I have no choice but to recommend that he go to a higher level. When he refuses, I am secretly glad. I give him extra homework, he writes me long letters, which I read and correct, and his progress continues at the same fast rate.

When he asks to see me outside class and I tell him no, he blames his poor English. If I understood Russian, I would not turn him down, he is utterly sure of that. The better his English, the better his chances with me. So he works and works, until he is way ahead of his classmates. Over their heads, he and I hit the ball, our

talk full of the double entendres that are the heart of flir-
tation.

About his own progress he later says: "I did it only for
you, because I knew I have only a little time, and I study,
study, study, because I want to—to—"

I teach him the word *seduce.*

He laments that he cannot do his seducing in
Russian—a richer language than English, he insists, better
for making love.

"I like to dream," he writes in one of his letters.
"Because in dreams you can have all what you want." He
says that he often dreams of going back to Odessa and
taking me along as his wife.

In my own dream he stays married, takes me as a lover,
and teaches me Russian.

Thirty-seven years old and already two years a grandfather. A not uncommon Russian story. Married at twenty, he
became husband and father at once, for his wife had a two-
year-old son by another marriage. "We meet first time on
tram." Of course: "I wanted son of my own blood." But:
"When I went to place where my daughter born" (Russian
style, the father is nowhere near the mother when she gives
birth), "and they tell me she girl, I run out from that place."
The grudge against mother and daughter lasted for years.
He had little feeling for this baby girl who did nothing but
"all time cry." But once she outgrew her infancy everything
changed. Telling the story, he makes small clutching and
clinging gestures, he imitates her childish cry: "Father,
Father." She got her message across. "From that time I begin
to love her, and I always love her since." Now Svetlana is fif-

teen and: "She has my head. Mother's face, but my head." Proud. He has high hopes for his girl. Only a few months in this country, she is doing well in school, and her English is as good as his. "She will go to college, no doubt about it."

Mother is a different story. She speaks no English at all and she will not learn it.

Yet another marriage doomed—it seems to me, at least—from the start.

Right after the wedding, Vadim moves into the single room where his wife and stepson have been living with her parents. A newlywed's hell. At night, only a curtain separates the beds. Though Vadim and his wife hardly dare to breathe, the father complains every morning about the creaking mattress, how it disrupts his sleep. Between Vadim and his wife's people there will always be trouble. In time, husband and father-in-law come to blows. More than once the police are called in to restore peace. Vadim insists that his wife's people do not like him because he is Russian. In Russia, he says, every Jewish joke is about the stupidity of Russians. He blames a lot of the problems of his marriage on race. "It is mistake to marry other race, now I see it," he says. Homesick, he never forgets that it is because his wife is Jewish that they have come to the United States.

One last hard drunken brawl ends with the father-in-law falling down dead. Murder? An autopsy shows a cerebral hemorrhage. Enough to clear Vadim in the eyes of the law, but not in the hearts of his wife's family.

Incredibly, no one thinks of divorce. And now, many years later, family history repeats itself, in a Brooklyn housing project. Vadim and his wife and their daughter, his stepson and *his* wife and their two-year-old boy, and Vadim's mother-in-law, all squeezed into the powder keg of a small one-bedroom apartment. The very windows hum with the tension. Vadim and his mother-in-law have exchanged hardly a word since her husband's death. Daily fights between Vadim and his wife. "She scream and scream." He says that when he runs into his neighbors, who are all Russians too, and who can understand every word, they look at him with disgust. Since there are more people living in that apartment than the lease allows, it is folly to draw attention to themselves. And so Vadim sees his wife's refusal to lower her voice as a sign of madness. But she will not be shut up. And what does she scream? That Vadim is no good, that he is ugly and useless, and that his penis is too small. Be all that as it may, she is his wife. No matter how bad the fighting gets, she always does her work. Always food on the table, a tidy house, clean clothes. Every penny Vadim earns he turns over to her, and when he needs money for something he must get it from her. How strange, I think, but: "It is Russian style."

Money. As always, the first order of business. How to make a living in the new country. In the beginning there is help: welfare, food stamps, free medical care, free English classes. (Hard to imagine how my students could do without such help, though of course my own parents had to do without it.) Repeated attempts to find work at the Brooklyn Marine Terminal come to nothing, and Vadim begins training to drive a cab. The owner of a Queens garage pays for his training, and in return Vadim must work for him for two months. (On his first day of work, he calls me from the street: "Are you free now? I wanted to take you for walk in my cab.") At first he does not know the city, where and when to get fares. He works the night shift, and in the small hours sometimes cruises for miles without finding a fare. As a new hire he is not permitted to work Friday or Saturday nights, the best nights for business. Almost impossible to make much more than the $120 a night he must pay the garage for the use of the cab. Counting his money in the ash-pink dawn, he sees that, after ten hours, he has made only a few dollars for himself. More drivers than cars at his garage. Some days he goes to work and waits up to five hours for a car before giving up and going back home.

He sees an ad in the Russian newspaper: asbestos workers, thirty dollars an hour. "Oh, you don't want to do that!" But it is like trying to warn the Russians against swimming in the waters of Brighton Beach. ("Cleaner than Black Sea," they insist.) Vadim says, "If I must be afraid of everything I cannot live." He smokes four packs of Marlboros a day. What's a little asbestos? Both of his parents died in their early fifties, his mother just weeks after Vadim left for America. ("Today I received big sorrow," he wrote on his homework. "My mother is no more.") It was the hardships of Soviet life that killed them, Vadim believes. "I will not live long either. I have maybe ten, maybe fifteen years," he says. Calm.

But as it turns out, like so many ads for jobs in the immigrant papers, this one is a scam. To get the job you must have training, and to get that training you must pay a fee. When he goes to apply for this job, Vadim strikes up a conversation with a supervisor, who is Polish. They speak half in English, half in Russian. Vadim asks him what the chances are of getting the job after paying the fee of four hundred dollars. The Pole answers honestly. Vadim thanks him and leaves.

Before his obligation to the garage that paid for his training has been fulfilled, Vadim moves on. He has met another Odessan who lives in his neighborhood and who has his own cab. The owner agrees to let Vadim have the cab every other day. Vadim can keep it for twenty-four hours and drive whatever times he wants. Most days he sets out at dawn and drives between ten and fifteen hours, and on a good day manages to earn about three hundred dollars, half of which goes to the cab's owner and to pay for gas. By this time: "I know city like palm of my hand."

But there are bad days too. Very soon he is robbed. "Where did it happen?" "Amsterdam and One-oh-two." "One hundred-and-second." This gets a laugh. "I get robbed with gun, and you can think only to correct my English."

It is summer now, and I find myself often thinking of him, putting in over two hundred miles a day, not using the air conditioner so as to conserve gas ("I tell passengers it broke"), while my friends and I discuss the difficulties of making ends meet, over frozen margaritas in SoHo. My students never go to bars or restaurants. Most of them have eaten in a restaurant only once or twice in their lives. They try not to go anywhere that costs money. They hardly ever go to the movies, but they all have television, and they all have seen *The Terminator*. ("Arnold Schwarzenegger. He is your minister of culture, yes?" one student asks.)

Every day, when he goes off to work, Vadim's wife packs him two sandwiches and one or two pieces of fruit.

He eats these sometime during the day, and that is all he eats, because he is too tired to eat when he gets home from work. Soon he has lost ten pounds. Stopping for a meal during working hours is a luxury he would never allow himself. But going without cigarettes, expensive though they are, is just as unthinkable.

By now he has been in America for four months. The English course in which I taught him has come to an end. He is the first one in the class to find a job. Most of the others are still on welfare. And so will they be for a long time to come. Many for the rest of their lives, predicts Vadim. Disdainful.

Though he is proud to have found a job, he makes no secret of how much he loathes it. He is appalled at the whistling doormen of Park Avenue. "You know what I do to someone in Odessa if he whistle for me?" He stacks his fists and twists them in opposite directions—a gesture that he uses all the time but that never fails to unnerve me. But here: "Nothing I can do. I am nobody in this country. I must be as nigger here." The whistles are only a means of getting the drivers' attention, I suggest. But Vadim scoffs. "All doorman has to do is put out his hand and all drivers will see him. No. People whistle for you because they want to make you feel like dog."

In spite of everything, he never loses his humor. He is easily amused, he is a good talker, and he likes to tell stories about what happens on the job.

"Black man get in my cab, light up marijuana and say, 'Russian, eh? So, how do you like black people?'"

He is convinced—and what immigrant isn't?—that all Americans are crazy. The man who says he prefers to sit up front, then offers Vadim ten dollars to pull out his cock. The women who leave business cards with their tips: "Call me if you want to practice your English." (American women are not shy, I tell him. "But in Russia only a whore would do it so.") The young man who obviously has money but whose jeans are all holes. The foxy blond who turns out to be a man. The dog walker who hails a cab to go one block home, because his dog got tired. Vadim discovers that many New Yorkers are fascinated to meet a Russian. "Are you really from Russia?" "Yes, really." For the hundredth time. "You may touch me if you want." The Barnard student, a Russian major, who chats in nearly perfect Russian and leaves twenty dollars for a three-dollar fare.

One day he makes an illegal left onto Fifth Avenue. A policeman sees him. Vadim thinks he is dreaming when he gets out of the cab and hears the cop shout *"Ne dvigatsya!"* Every New York cop must have to learn this one Russian phrase: Don't move.

"But how did he know I am Russian?"

Making small talk with his passengers, or eavesdropping on their conversations, he picks up more English. "What means *take it easy*?" "What means *actually*? Why everyone use this word all time?" I tell him that *actually* is one of those words that can't be explained, but he will understand it after he's heard it enough times. And sure enough one day I find this message on my answering machine: "I know what means *actually* now!"

In the beginning, before he has learned his way around, he announces to each passenger: "I am new to this city and I only begin this job. Can you tell me, please, how to get there?" Most people are patient. But one old woman going to Central Park West throws up her hands in disgust. "What business do you have driving a cab if you don't know where you are going?"

"I say, Oh, listen, how do you think? I drive cab to feed my family. Believe me, I don't do it to annoy you." He hits the gas then, and soon—"like so many my passengers"—she is shrieking at him to slow down. "'Slow down! Slow down!' Why they all want me to slow down? Do they think I don't know how to drive? No, I say them, I cannot slow down, I must make money. I don't understand. This woman, for example. She must be eighty, maybe ninety years old, but she *cling* to life." He shakes his head. "I don't understand."

No, he wouldn't understand. He is not afraid of anything. He is not afraid to drive a cab at night, without a partition, even after he's been robbed. He is not afraid to drive to any neighborhood, at any hour.

"Why do I have to be afraid? If my God want me to die right now, I die. If he want me to live, I live. You are like my wife, afraid of everything, I feel it all time. But then you are woman, it must be so. But my daughter is different, she is like me, she is not afraid of anything. She has my head, my blood."

Driving in the cab with him, I see it for myself: precisely that combination of recklessness and expertise that I would have predicted. But something puzzles me, and as we career through the streets I have to ask myself: Why is it that the collisions he so skillfully avoids make me feel safer and in better hands than I would feel were he to drive slowly and sanely?

I know this: He is the only truly fearless person I have ever met. And his fearlessness is part of the spell that binds me. "You are safe with me," he says. I want to believe him. "You don't have to be afraid of anything when I am near you."

I believe him.

The first time I see him without his shirt, I see the scars. On the insides of his arms, on his midriff; one curved like an eyebrow above the nipple-eye of his left breast. "Odessa. It is life in Odessa. Always trouble, always fighting. In Odessa, I was as an animal." This is not the moment to correct the preposition, so I refrain. He says something in Russian that doubtless translates as dog eat dog, or kill or be killed.

The biggest scar is on the inside of his left arm, between elbow and wrist. "I was tired from everything," is all he will say.

The oldest man I have ever been to bed with. The skin of his body is beautiful, tight and smooth, a decade younger than the skin of his face. Leggy blue-black spider climbs his arm. The crucifix keeps getting caught in my mouth.

On his body: "I am nothing now. But when I was twenty I was perfect man. I was sportsman, very strong. But then drugs . . . drink . . . "

Another question I ask myself a lot: Had I known everything about him, would I have resisted? (I *did* resist at first. I told him it was inappropriate for me to see him outside class. Impossible. School rules. Not to mention his being married. Impossible? He knew better. How? He says that after his first declaration of love—he managed to work a declaration of love into almost every homework—he noticed that I avoided meeting his eyes during class. His interpretation: She likes me too. It was so. But if I had known everything about him, would I have kept on resisting?)

"I was big drugger in Odessa."

Vocabulary lesson. I teach him *addict, junkie, needle, habit, shoot up, get high, OD.*

About a year before coming to America, he tried the popular at-home cure: Knock yourself out with sleeping pills for a couple of weeks. It worked and it didn't work. He could not resist shooting up a few more times before leaving Odessa, and in New York it is only a matter of time before the right (or wrong, I should say) passenger gets in his cab. In the way of these things, they know each other instantly (as I suppose we did too). They drive to East Harlem. ("That room. It was very interesting for me to see. Because it was the same like in Odessa. Empty room, one table, chair. Cards on table. Just the same. Druggers are the same everywhere." He scores a gram of cocaine and goes home "to cook it." He has never done coke before. It is not at all the high he expects but he has no regrets. He shrugs off my fears. "I just wanted to taste American drugs, but I am not going to get habit again. Now I have to work hard and make money, I can't think about drugs. Maybe later."

He tells me stories about the crazy things addicts he knew back in Odessa would try. Spread a little shoe polish on a piece of bread. Let sit a few hours. Scrape off the crud. Eat the bread. You'll get a buzz. Shoe polish and insecticide can also be rubbed into the scalp. You shave a little patch on your crown and pull a plastic bag over your head to speed up the effect. Vadim is contemptuous of such desperate measures. Drugs are for fun, to make yourself feel good. How can you feel good doing something like this? Even when he didn't have the money to buy drugs, it was easy enough to drive into the country and steal the poppies yourself; they were not hard to find, blooming illegally between rows of conveniently tall corn. It was risky business: You could get shot in those fields. But the fields of East Harlem are dangerous too. Vadim can handle it. ("If I have to be afraid of everything, I cannot live.")

He finds another dealer, closer to home, through an attendant at a gas station he uses, and soon he is shooting up once or twice a week: sometimes coke, sometimes heroin, often both. He doesn't want his arms to be covered with telltale tracks, as they were in Odessa, so he shoots into the veins of his hands and wrists. One of the scars on his right arm is from an old infection caused by a dirty needle. Now he is scrupulous about keeping his needle clean.

And from what I can tell, so far at least, drugs have been less harmful to Vadim than his other demon. Like no small number of Russian men, he is able to chug an entire bottle of vodka. Russian style. Two bottles a night, no problem. He was often drunk. And when he was drunk he was often violent. So many close calls with knives and cars, he might have been a cat. But before he could use up all of his lives his wife took things in hand. For once the two enemies, Vadim's wife and Vadim's mother, saw eye to eye. Before he left for America, he had to get clean. He kicked the drugs on his own, but for alcohol they dragged him to a doctor.

The first thing this doctor made him do was sign a paper absolving the doctor from responsibility. Vadim was then told to open his mouth, which the doctor filled with spray from an aerosol can. Vadim had to hold the liquid under his tongue a few minutes before swallowing. Shortly after he swallowed, his skin turned fiery, his temperature soared but soon dropped back to normal and he was himself again. That's it, said the doctor. You can go home. But by this simple means a cure had been worked. Were Vadim to start drinking again any time in the next five years, he would die.

A hard-to-believe story. First of all I want to know whether this doctor knew about the suicide attempt Vadim had made. Surely his wife and his mother knew about it? For his part Vadim finds it hard to believe that I have never heard of this cure, so well-known in his country. Some people choose to have an ampule of the drug injected into their flesh, but Vadim had shied away from this method, said to be riskier than the aerosol spray. (It is the first time I hear him speak of a risk he deemed *not* worth taking.)

But do people who drink after this treatment really die? I am skeptical about the whole business. Vadim says he knows of people who drank and died, but he knows of others who drank and survived. You could never be sure. More Russian roulette. For the moment he himself is playing it safe. But is he cured? He does not seem so to me, at least not in the twelve-step way that we would understand. If you asked me, I'd say he was only waiting to get that five-year sentence behind him.

His wife often screams at the top of her lungs, "You are nothing but a no-good drugger!" To her husband, further proof of her insanity. "Why she want to tell everyone about it? In Russia she scream like this, and in Russia, believe me, people think very badly of druggers." I warn him that people in Brooklyn have their prejudices too. Vadim's wife does not drink or smoke or take drugs. More than a touch of regret when he reports this. Life is more fun when others share our vices. "Will you shooting with me sometime?" he asks with a kiss. And yet he is displeased when I mention once that I'd drunk too much at a bar the night before. Nothing worse than a woman drunk in public, he tells me—oh so Russian. He is not pleased when I light up a cigarette either. Of course, it would have been one of the things he adored about his wife when they met: her clean living. The sinful are always moved by the love of the pure.

He carries a photograph in his wallet. "Mother, Father, and I." Mother is plain, Father handsome as a dream. And Father it is who holds the child—their only child (who didn't let *his* father down by being a girl)—holds him off to one side, so that Mother has to crane her neck to see. They are both gazing down at their son, concealed in a dark blanket that appears remarkably coarse—burlap, it looks like. Completely concealed: no small fist sticking up, no adorably rounded baby brow.

I can get almost nothing out of him about his parents. Of his father he will say only: "My father was not my father, he was my friend." Of his mother: "She thought only about me." Perfect parents, in other words. I don't say what I think, which is that if your parents were perfect you do not grow up as an animal, you do not become an alcoholic and a junkie, or grow so sick of living by the age of thirty that you try to kill yourself. But Mother and Father are dead, and I am touched by Vadim's loyalty. (And if parent-bashing is out, there is always the Communist party. For every hardship of his life Vadim blames the Communist party.)

His father was wounded by shellfire in two separate actions during the Second World War—that war that Vadim informs me was won by Russians, with only a little American help. (Out of respect for twenty million Russian dead, I hold my tongue.)

Drink was his father's demon too, and if he had another addiction it was women. "My father was like me. He always had a lot of women. He could not live without it." I want to know what his mother thought about that. Vadim says he doesn't know. But were your parents happy? I persist. He says he cannot court them. Judge them, you mean. Yes, sorry: judge them. He smiles. You always could understand me.

You always could understand me. He says this to me all the time. You always could understand me. Tender. Grateful. His English may be broken but he is safe with me. That I am the one who taught him English—our common language, and the language of survival in the new country—is something he never forgets. But the closer I become to him the stronger my desire to speak to him in his own language, and to have him be the one to teach it to me. Impractical. Between his job and his family Vadim has never had much time for me, and much of the time we are together we are silent. When would we study Russian? You are always hearing people say things like, "I learned French in cafés and in the street," "I learned English in bed," but I don't know what they are talking about. The only way I know of learning a language is by studying—hard and methodically.

Vadim also wishes that I spoke Russian. He has dreams in which I appear speaking it fluently, as I used to appear in my own dreams speaking German. To think that neither my father nor my mother ever showed any desire to teach me his or her language. A terrible withholding, that now seems to me.

Love and language. The immigrants speak of the pain they feel when their children insist on speaking only in English. Disdain for the mother tongue: a plague among the immigrant youth. "When my son speak to me in English," one Korean man says, "it is knife to my heart."

There are teenagers in Vadim's neighborhood, friends of his daughter's, who were born in Brooklyn of Russian parents and who speak almost no Russian, while their parents speak almost no English. How can they understand each other? But I know a Chinese-American man who grew up speaking no Chinese, though that was his mother's only language. *Somehow* she raised him.

He is smart, my Vadim. He was my best student. "Vadim is polyglot," one of his classmates used to say. But it wasn't easy for him to learn English. He had to work hard. He worked harder than all the rest. Even after our class had ended, when most of the others simply gave up, he kept working. Studying his dictionary while waiting in line in his cab at the airport. Practicing with his passengers, asking them questions, getting them to help him. At night, before falling asleep, he holds imaginary dialogues with me in his head. At home, of course, and almost everywhere in his neighborhood, only Russian is spoken. I am the only native American he knows. "You *are* my America," he says.

Someone's America—me!

Constantly fretting over his inadequate English—or is it English itself that is inadequate? So much weaker and blander than Russian, English seems to him. Wherever the fault lies, all he knows is that he cannot express himself fully. If only I knew Russian! Yes, I must learn it, and quickly too. For unless I know Russian, how can he describe how he feels about me?

He says, "Caress me, beloved." He says, "I very love you." And: "When you put your head on my breast, my heart runs out of me."

Whenever I praise his English he says, "I did it for you." Not the whole truth, of course, but it cannot be denied: He studied hard for me.

"My dear, can I say, 'I dote on you'? It is correct?" "Can I say, 'I adore you'?" "I search my dictionary for ways to tell you."

My heart runs out of me.

In all those years, my father never learned enough English to tell me how he felt about me.

➵

Father and son had much in common. Father worked all his life for the Odessa port too, doing exactly the same work the son would eventually do, though he was never held back in his job, as Vadim would be, for having married a Jewish woman. Father and son both drank a lot and smoked a lot, and they both married very young and had one child, and they both fucked around incessantly. A father who, on occasion, when procuring a woman for himself, had procured one for his son too, which may be one of the things Vadim meant when he said his father was not his father but his friend.

I want to know about the women but Vadim says there is nothing to tell. "I don't remember them. I did not love them. It was nature for me to want them, because I am man, but I did not care about them. I wanted only one thing from them, and after it I was saying, Get away from me."

And not a hint of shame in those blue wolf's eyes.

Was I wrong, or did I detect a change, a slight diminution of passion, once we had become lovers? Often it seemed to me that for Vadim much of the thrill might have been in the chase. I knew he wasn't just boasting when he said, "I wish everything I want in life was as easy for me to get as woman." Had he thought (hoped?) that I (the American, the schoolteacher) would be more of a challenge? In the beginning, there was something almost fearful to me about his tension—that way the expert seducer has of convincing you that he will suffer something dire if you don't give in to him. *Nervous, hungry,* and *tormented* were words he used to describe himself. And: "You must make up your mind about me soon, because I cannot stand it, I am like dog in box!" Once we had become lovers, though, all the anxiety seemed to fall away. A calm descended. More attractive to me than ever was he calm, and it was I who became nervous, hungry, and tormented.

I want to know about his wife. Olga the ogress. "I don't

love her and she doesn't love me." He is always threatening to leave. She is always begging him to stay. Why, if she doesn't love him? "Because she is like dog on harvest." What? "It is Russian saying." Surely something amiss in the translation, but I get it ("You always could understand me!"): When a person doesn't want something, but doesn't want anyone else to have it either.

It was his wife's idea to come to the States. Vadim, who says he never had any desire to leave his homeland, jumped at this chance. His wife cried for days when he told her she should go to America without him. How could she go without him? How would she get by in the new country? Who would support her and her mother and daughter? That was a man's job, she reminded him. There was her son who would be going along, but Volodya, though just out of his teens, already had his own wife and child. "She was right. She would be lost here without me. In the end I could not spit on her." And now, he says, "I am alone. I am really all alone in this country." What can he mean? Doesn't he live with his family? Doesn't he live in Little Odessa, surrounded by brother Russians? "No Russians," he says. "Only Jewish." His wife's people are not his people. "In family, only I and my daughter are Russian." What? Svetlana is Russian, Vadim explains, because she has a Russian father. But to Olga Svetlana is Jewish. He has Russian law on his side, she has Jewish law on hers. But the laws don't matter, Vadim says. "All you have to do is spend five minutes with my girl to know she is Russian." Simple test.

Both Volodya's natural father and Volodya's wife are Jewish.

Unlike Olga, Vadim had no friends or family to welcome him here, and he can think only of those he left behind and whom he may never see again. Something else to hold over his wife's head. "She is not homesick. She does not suffer. Only I."

Who is right about nostalgia? Goethe, who cursed it as useless and morbid? Or Herder, for whom it was "the noblest of all pains"? I don't know, but I always suspected that it was as much for Vadim's sake as for her own that Olga wanted to get away from Odessa. Hadn't he said himself that he lived like an animal there, always in trouble, always fighting? Perhaps Olga believed that America could tame him. A new land, a new life, a second chance for both of them. If that was her hope she was to be disappointed. Vadim says that when she came home one evening to find him nodding in the dark, and she turned on the light and saw those bloodshot eyes, she clutched her head with both hands and backed away from him screaming.

Vadim doesn't believe his wife was thinking about him. He says she never thinks about him, she thinks only about herself. And: "She keep me only because she need money, and she doesn't want to be alone, without man." I say what seems to me obvious, but Vadim sets me straight. "Here in America you can be forty and still young. But we are Russian and we are not young. My wife is old woman, she is grandmother. She is not going to find other man now."

Olga loves America—or at least *her* America, which means Little Odessa. Not the housing project, of course, where things have changed only for the worse since I was a girl, and the talk is still all about getting out. (If it is true that many Americans have had to let go of the dream of one day owning a home, the immigrants still cling to it fiercely.)

Olga is thrilled with American stores. All the many kinds of stores, with never an empty rack or shelf—nothing like this in the Old Country. "She and my daughter, they shop and shop." But since they can't afford to buy much, it is mostly window shopping. They like to look and to touch and to dream. To Vadim it is ridiculous. "Why I have to come to America for this?" About one thing, though, he and his wife agree. They did the best thing they could have done for their daughter. "Here, she can go to college, she can be anything. She can have all what she wants." Vadim is always happy when he speaks of his daughter. His faith in her future is unshakable. But doesn't he ever worry about being a bad influence? The suggestion only amuses him. "No, believe me, one thing I know for sure, my daughter will never be a drugger. Because she see what happen to me in Odessa, and she is not stupid. My daughter will never touch drugs." One good reason to think he may be right is his stepson, who hardly drinks, has never taken drugs, and is completely faithful to his wife. More than one way for a father to set an example. But later, when I have learned more about Vadim's past, I will think it nothing short of miraculous that his children have grown up all right. I don't think it was luck, though. I think it was Olga.

Vadim gets angry when he discovers that all the money he has earned and handed over to his wife is gone. He is trying to save. He wants to buy his own cab, or some kind of business, like a laundromat, as soon as possible. "I must think about future. I do not want to drive taxi for rest of my life." He hears about another apartment, bigger, in a better neighborhood, and with a nice low rent. The people who live there now are willing to pass on the lease for a fee of ten thousand dollars. To think he can save that kind of money on his salary seems unrealistic to me. But he has the shining example of the man for whom he is working now, who drove a cab day and night for five years and managed to save ten times that. I had forgotten. Those spectacular feats of getting and not spending that are part of the immigrant story. It really is another America. I try to think of anyone else I know who saves money. But all my friends are always spending, always broke, up to the limit on their credit cards, behind in their payments, dissatisfied with their jobs and their salaries, and always complaining. Of course they would like to have more money, but they would never work hours and hours at some lowly job to get it. One hundred thousand dollars. I don't think I could save that in a lifetime, let alone five years.

Whenever we talk on the phone Vadim has his dictionary handy. One day when we are talking about his wife (once again he has decided to leave her), he says, "My wife is very—very—wait." Rustle of pages. "Coarse? Rude?" "Gruff," I suggest. "Yes, yes, rough. My wife is very rough. It is not good for me. I need a woman who is—" Rustle, rustle. I can guess the word before he finds it. "Tender."

Was Olga never tender? Was there never a time when they were happy together? Vadim thinks back. Soon after their marriage, he took a job that brought him to the Far East, to Vladivostok, and Olga went with him. Vladivostok. One of those faraway lands with delicious names (Zanzibar was another) that I hardly believed really existed when I was a child, in those days before I knew how small the world really was. Vladivostok. Zanzibar. Pago Pago.

"And that time was really not bad," Vadim admits. But that was eighteen years ago.

He was still a teenager when he first met Olga. And did he want to get married right away? "Yes, of course. It is Russian style." And Olga, with one bad marriage already behind her, and a child—

I can see them: the tall young smiling sailor with the blue, blue eyes and the helpless fair young mother.

Olga never loved her first husband, supposedly. She married him only because her parents, who were friends of his parents, bullied her into it.

I ask Vadim to give me photographs and this makes him uneasy. He is afraid that I want the photographs because I am planning to leave him. This is astute: I am always planning to leave him. (Once, he said to me, "I don't know why you love me. I am married, I am poor, I am drinker, I am drugger—" *I am lunatic,* the answer came to me. But I still hoped to come to my senses.)

Here he is in black and white, in bathing trunks, tense and unsmiling, just before a race. He wasn't lying. He really was perfect.

It is from photographs of his daughter that I form my image of his wife, since Vadim has said that Svetlana has her mother's face. And certainly I can see nothing of him in that pretty round face with the dark round eyes and dark flowing hair. So he chose a wife who was his opposite physically too, and not really his type. (Early on, I had said to him, "What do you want with me? I am not your type.

You like blonds with big tits." "How did you know this?" Genuine surprise. Then: "It is true. If my friends in Odessa know I love woman so small, they laugh at me, they don't believe it.")

But it turns out Olga is a blond. It happened soon after they met. When she discovered that Vadim liked blonds, she began to bleach her hair. Through all the changes the marriage has suffered since, she still bleaches her hair— just as he still wears the mustache that he grew way back then, at Olga's request.

I am the first woman Vadim has ever known to use tampons. "In Russia women use—*kak eto*?" He mimes the wringing out of a wet rag. He tells me how, when he took his daughter to register for school, the woman doing the paperwork asked about Sveta's periods. Vadim had to translate for his daughter, who was mortified. "Russian people are very shy," he says.

"We don't have sex, we only have children," Russians make fun of themselves. THERE IS NO SEX IN RUSSIA, reads a popular button.

Vadim clarifies. "There is a lot of sex in Russia, and a lot of dirty sex, but it is all outside the home."

One long afternoon in bed we teach each other the dirty words.

In Russia they say having sex with a condom is like kissing through a handkerchief.

Cheating is known as going to the left.

The Soviet Union: the pro-lifer's worst nightmare, the highest abortion rate in the world. At clinics you have to stand in line for your abortion, just as you do to buy milk or bread. Not unusual for a woman to have ten or more.

Vadim thinks his wife has had closer to twenty. I am surprised that he doesn't know the exact number, but then I remember: A husband who is not there when you give birth to his child is not likely to keep up with your abortions. And why aren't Russian men there when their wives give birth? Vadim shrugs. "Why I want to be there? This is no place for man."

Twenty abortions. No anesthetic.

Russian women can do anything. Russian women are tractors. These are popular sayings too.

Often now when I think of Olga I see her as Vadim described her that time: clutching her head between her hands, backing away, screaming.

"You don't have to feel sorry for Russian women." Vadim assures me that the relationship between the sexes is much happier in Russia than in America. He with his immigrant cabbie's view: "Here women all crazy and men all gay."

Homosexuality, like pornography, was illegal in the Old Country.

If for no other reason, Olga is better off than I because she has a husband. Vadim does not believe me when I say I don't want to marry. "What will you do when you are old? I think of you in ten, twenty years. It will be terrible, terrible." In Russia I could have no worse fate. Never to marry, to be an old maid: the worst shame upon a Russian woman.

Any sympathy I express for Olga amuses Vadim. "Believe me, if she knew about you she would kill you," he says, finally achieving the conditional.

Already she has her suspicions. Vadim's hair has grown

over his ears, and though he is usually fastidious about haircuts, he keeps putting off going to the barber. And she is sensitive to his moods. "What are *you* so happy about?" Standing in front of him with her hands on her hips, glaring, suspicious. I know this woman.

But the really solid evidence is the missing money. Olga knows how much her husband ought to be bringing home, and some days he is way short. She doesn't buy his stories about there being no passengers or the cab breaking down. That missing money can mean only one of two things: drugs or a woman.

One day, right after she leaves the house, he calls me. We are talking, he is rustling through his dictionary, he doesn't hear her sneaking back into the house. We don't hear her picking up the extension in the kitchen. She holds her breath and she listens. No English, but she understands. When she can bear it no more she begins screaming in Russian. I can hear her through both phones, as if there were two of her screaming. I am about to hang up when she switches to English—"English teacher, hah!"— and spits into the receiver.

Now, whenever their phone rings and the caller hangs up, Olga says, "It's your American prostitute!"

(Once, Vadim calls while I am out, and a friend who happens to be visiting me answers. "Didn't say who he was," she reports. "But I'd swear it was Count Dracula.")

Olga doesn't want to know anything about me. She knows it all already. Whoever I am I can only be of the same low breed as he. Like to like. Who else would want him? Scum to scum. We deserve each other.

When Vadim confesses to her that he is in love, she faints.

I don't see him for over a week. Later he will describe Olga's carrying on. Crying, screaming, vomiting, fainting. Taking to her bed, calling her mother and her daughter to her. Begging Svetlana to help, to bring her father to his senses. Oh, who will save them! Vadim cries too, when he describes his daughter sobbing on his neck, his mother-in-law falling to her knees. (A man who cries readily and without shame—something I have not known before. Tears sometimes choke Vadim when we are making love.)

He says, "My dear, forgive me, but I don't know what I can do." Does this mean he loves Olga, after all? "I pity her. Because it is true, she will be lost in this country without me." And how is Olga doing now? "She is better. She tries very hard to change herself. She does not scream so much, and she is calm. Now she tries to do everything very nice for me."

For the first time in a long while they are having sex. For the first time in years Olga is tender.

I pull the arrow from my breast and break it over my knee. "I can scream and faint too, you know."

I am beside myself when he gets his hair cut.

He says, "Beloved, you know I want only to be with you but I cannot spit on my family. But I worry about you, what will happen to you, because I see now what you are tormented." And: "My dear, you know I love you and will always love you, but sometimes I think maybe it were better if we never meet."

I want to be there when he finally gets the past conditional.

Pity was a big word with Vadim. He was always pitying someone. Sometimes after we made love he looked at me with what I thought was pity. Or knew, rather. It was pity all right. But why did he pity me?

He said often: "I can be very ugly." (But never in warning; he never once threatened me.)

He gives me a telephone number. "Ask for Sasha. He doesn't know English, but if you say to him only 'I need Vadim,' he will understand, he will call to me and I will call to you." I assumed that this Sasha was a friend of Vadim's and could hardly believe it when I found out that he was Olga's younger brother. Wasn't Vadim worried that Sasha would tell Olga? Vadim says no, Sasha would never do that, "because he is afraid of me. You have not seen it, but he has seen it. I can be crazy. I can be very ugly." And I remembered what Vadim had done to Sasha and Olga's father.

It was always hard for me to imagine how Vadim must be with his wife. One day he tells me a story that helps me to see them as a couple, and to see him through her eyes.

He came home one night to find Olga waiting up for him. She was very upset. Earlier that day she had witnessed her son beating his little boy and she had tried to stop him. She reminded Volodya that Vadim had never beaten him when he was a child. But, instead of being ashamed, her son had turned on her and begun to berate her. She was still trembling when she told Vadim the story. If you had been home, it would never have happened, she said. Volodya would never have beaten their grandchild, and he would never have dared to speak to his mother that way.

Was Vadim a good man? A bad man? Was he a bad husband? Was he a good or a bad father?

In Odessa Vadim had a dog. Among the photographs he shows me is one of himself with the dog, a broad-chested Alsatian wearing a muzzle. Why the muzzle? Without it, says Vadim, the dog was very dangerous. I tell him the sad story of my own big dog, whom I had to give away, because he kept attacking other dogs and I was not strong enough to hold him. Vadim says it was because I had not trained my dog properly. "You must beat them every day when they are young."

Now I have a cat. He is old and mean. I warn visitors not to touch him, but some of them ignore this and end up badly scratched.

"I like the animals and they like me," Vadim says, stroking the cat, who has climbed into his lap.

If I spoke the same language as that cat, I would like to tell him what Vadim told me: how, back in Odessa, whenever his own cat had kittens, he would drown them. "They don't feel anything," he insists. "I put them in sock and drown them in bathtub."

At the English language school the teachers are required to include lessons on hygiene. Students are told that Americans take showers every day and always wear deodorant. "Deadorant" is how one of my students spells it. Imagine doing the same thing at the UN, with the diplomats who come from the same countries as our students. But it is only immigrants who are assumed to need lessons in washing. In the teachers' lounge you often hear remarks about how the students smell. I want to tell everyone that Vadim does not smell. He washes. He is clean.

But—he throws empty cigarette packs and other trash in

the street! When I protest he says, "Someone will pick up later. This is job for someone."

Midnight, and we are parked in his cab in front of my apartment building. Vadim is drinking a Coke. When the Coke is all gone, he tosses the can out the window. It bounces three times, then rolls clatteringly, the noise resounding in the empty street. A few of my neighbors, out with their dogs, turn and frown. Vadim is unaware. I sink low in my seat.

And I want to sink through the ground when I find out that he cheats his passengers. Foreigners, of course, are the easiest victims. "I must do it," he says. "I must make more money. I have to get something for myself in this country. You would do same."

He laughs when I tell him people are supposed to tip him at least fifteen percent. "Many people give me one nickel, one dime."

A cheat. A litterbug. A drowner of kittens.

I don't want to condemn him. I want to understand everything, imagining that the more I understand, the less he will be guilty. That old fallacy.

When he sees someone on crutches, or an elderly person struggling along, he stops the cab and offers him or her a free ride. Very few people accept. "They don't trust me. Because Americans cannot trust each other. Americans don't help each other. Russians are different. Russians have a wide soul. But when they come in America, Russians change. They become like Americans. They don't want to help. Especially they don't want to help the new immigrants."

He gives change or a cigarette to anyone who asks.

Things come back to me—things learned in the great, enchanted country of Russian books. About Russian pity and Russian cruelty and Russian fatalism. And things learned first from my mother, about Russian love of country and Russian rape. ("Every woman in Berlin. Even old women and children.") Women and men alike fleeing before the Red soldiers at the end of the war. (And would it all be repeated in my own lifetime, when they came to bury us and took over the world?)

The more Vadim tells me about his past, the less I want to hear. But how else can I understand him? I must know everything.

Back in Odessa he didn't just use drugs, he also sold them. Listening to him talk about the friends he left behind, it dawns darkly on me that he is talking not about just any circle of chums but about a gang. Dominant among them is one called Yuri. ("My best friend and a really good guy.") Jailed for twelve years for killing a man in a knife fight; killed in a knife fight twelve years later, just days after his release. ("First time was about woman, second time about drugs.")

"It was life in Odessa." An outlaw life, full of petty crime. Breaking and entering, car theft, banditry. Vadim speaks of it all lightly. "We were six in car, we stop bus, get on bus, take passengers' money, and run out."

And wasn't he ever caught? Yes, but thanks to a good connection in the KGB (an old war buddy of his father's), Vadim never had to go to jail. ("This is how it work in Russia. It take only one phone call.")

Did Olga know? "Of course. My wife know everything about me." And how did she respond? "She scream, like always. And I say her, Please, leave me rest now, because the police have broken my body." But she still didn't want a divorce.

A bad man. Degenerate. Incorrigible.

My friends want to know how I can go on seeing him. Nervous, timid me, who is afraid of everything. But I was never afraid of Vadim. I never saw him "ugly." He never showed that side to me.

I want to believe that he is a good man twisted—as you or I or anyone would be—by his circumstances. I want to blame everything on the bad deal life has cut him—on poverty, lack of education, Soviet benightedness, too much testosterone. He has never hit his children, I remind myself. He has never beaten his wife: I find myself clinging to this.

He takes his own fate as a victim in stride. About being mugged he says, "I can do same." *The same?* My heart is pounding. Does that mean he's going to rob people in his cab? He laughs. "No, of course not in cab." "But—you're going to mug people." "No, don't worry, I am not going to do it. I am not stupid. I don't have green card." "You need a green card to mug people." A bigger laugh. "I don't want to be deported."

I give it a try: Doesn't he think that the men who robbed him were wrong, and that he was wrong to rob other people, and that the world would be a better place if we didn't do this sort of thing unto one another?

But Vadim has his own spin on the golden rule: Today I am unlucky. Tomorrow it is someone else's turn to be unlucky.

Shameless. Impenitent.

When two apartments in my building are broken into, the suspicion has to cross my mind. It isn't likely—it is highly unlikely—but it could have been. . . .

After he is robbed a second time in his cab, Vadim gets a gun. "In Odessa knife is enough, but I see not here."

I study the bulletin board outside the teachers' lounge. English teachers wanted in Japan, in Turkey, in China, and in the Soviet Union.

A woman I know is having a baby. Another woman gives a shower for her in an apartment on the Upper West Side. I know most of the women who are invited. These are women I have worked with, women I went to school with. Friends.

A tea-shower. Embroidered napery, a grandmother's porcelain, an ornate Chinese teapot, like a miniature temple. Sandwiches and sweets. Ceremonious and charming. No one smokes.

The gifts have all been opened and admired and put aside. The afternoon is almost gone. Most of the guests have left, and among those lingering I find myself the center of attention, hot in the sunlight that pours through the window behind my chair. Here are women who are close to me, good women, friends, women who have been through things, who know what it is to be in trouble with a man, to be in over your head with a man, to love a man too much, past reason, and to no possible good to yourself. None of them has ever met Vadim, though I have shown them photographs, and I have spoken much about him.

They say: Why do you go on seeing him? Is it the danger? Is it the adventure, the risk that attracts you? Is it the sex?

"Is it his smell?" asks the woman who is going to have the baby (the woman with the ex-lover's shirt in the plastic bag in her bottom dresser drawer).

"It's because he's a foreigner, isn't it. It's because he is Russian. It's the accent."

"If he were American—an American dockworker, say— you wouldn't give him the time of day."

If he were an American dockworker, he would *tawk like dis,* it is true, and I'd be repelled. I try to imagine an American dockworker quoting Shakespeare, as Vadim has quoted Pushkin to me.

His accent, his broken speech, his slow acquiring of English—all this has certainly been important to me. It was language that brought us together, first of all, and it has always moved me to hear him speak. I would miss following his progress, being there when he no longer has to stammer and grope, when he can say anything he wants to say in English. This is serious stuff for me. I am shocked when I meet a man who says he is about to marry an Italian woman but has no intention of learning Italian. What kind of love is that? Ultimately, I decide against registering for a course in Russian, because I know what this would mean. I have no business learning Russian. I have to leave Vadim.

"Is it because he's bad? Is it the toughness and the violence that excite you?"

But I have never known toughness or violence from Vadim. A cliché: It is often the violent men who turn out to be the gentlest in bed. Still, it was the last thing I would have expected of him: this voluptuous tenderness. Another question: If it was only pleasure, why did we go about it as if it were the gravest business on earth? It wasn't the same for him, though. He never went as far, he was never as naked as I. It seemed to me that with him there remained always one last integument—thin, but intact. At that moment of greatest exposure, when you feel as if not only your clothes but your very skin had been peeled away, your greatest fear is that the other—the one responsible, the one who has brought you to this point—will look away. Vadim did not look away. Instead he looked harder than ever at me. That's when I saw that he pitied me.

"But don't you ever feel, well, you know—degraded? Disgusted with yourself?"

No. Never that.

"But what good can it come to? Even if he were free. What are you going to do, marry a cabbie?"

The assumption that I, that we all are better than Vadim, is not to be questioned.

"And don't forget, he *isn't* free. What about his wife? Think of what he's doing to her, and what you're doing to her. Women shouldn't cheat on each other like that."

"Not fair, not fair." (Several voices at once.) "It's the old double standard. Holding women to a higher moral code." "Not fair." "The same old bullshit."

There are days when I cannot get Olga off my mind. I know that Vadim has always been unfaithful to her, and that she has always suffered from this. But it seems to me that you had only to spend two minutes with Vadim to know what kind of man he was. You had only to look into those eyes to know that he would never be faithful to any woman. Hadn't Olga realized this too? She must have been full of love once upon a time, Olga. Full of hope.

Clutching her bleached blond hair in her fists, backing away, screaming.

("My wife say that my penis is too small. Tell me: This is true?")

"Hey, are you listening? We're talking to you. We're afraid for you. The guy is a junkie. A criminal. With a gun."

"How bad does he have to be? What does he have to do to make you come to your senses?"

"Why do they let people like that into the country anyway? Don't we have enough criminals?"

"He's bound to get into trouble again. Men like that don't change."

Vadim says that he already has changed. "I am not young anymore. I don't look for trouble." Yes, he still likes to get high now and then, it helps him relax, but he doesn't want to get addicted again, and he is not going to. He believes that if he works hard enough and saves enough money, he will be able "to get something for myself in this country." He says: "I promise you, I am not going to drive taxi for rest of my life." He says: "I want to work with my head." But what if things don't happen fast enough? Will he have the strength to keep struggling, or will he be overwhelmed? That would be an old story, wouldn't it: frustration—backsliding—drugs—crime. And if he gets caught, and if he's arrested? No KGB man is going to help him out here. I don't want to be around—

"Are you in love with him?"

No. I am not in love with Vadim. He holds some key, it is true. But it is not the key to my heart. He holds some answers for me—I can say this even without being able to say what the questions are. How can this be, when he knows nothing about me. I never talk about myself to him and he never asks questions. He is not curious about my life, about my background or my family or how I spend my days. He has no curiosity at all about me. After all, I am only a woman; facts about me can't be very important. (Remember what used to be meant by a woman's "vital statistics"?) But when he speaks I listen spellbound, I hang on every word, as if with the next will surely come that wisdom or knowledge about myself that I am convinced lies with him.

Everyone thinks that he's got me conned, that he is a villain and I am his victim. If this is true, why is it that my feelings toward him are never aggrieved ones? Why, on the contrary, do I feel guilty toward Vadim?

I often think about Svetlana. I imagine her in that crowded apartment, in the kitchen that smells of cabbage and onions—that smell that rises from the pages of so many Russian books—doing her homework at the kitchen table. In the next room, her mother and father are fighting. Oh, the things they say to each other! She will never get used to it, no matter how often she hears it. For the hundredth time she swears to herself that she will never ever marry. Already at fifteen she looks like a woman, and she has her pick of boys, to her father's anxiety. She knows her power and she will use it, she will have as many boys as she likes. But she will never marry.

Sometimes she hears her own name being screamed, hears her parents arguing about her, whether she is Russian or Jewish, *his* daughter or *her* daughter—and sometimes she gets up from the table and goes in to them and tells them they must stop, she cannot take any more. She who is so proud, who seldom cries, cannot hold back the tears as she pleads with them. She loves them both, and she is best friend to both of them. Confidant, go-between, peacemaker—she knows all these roles. Olga confides in Sveta about her marriage and counts on her daughter to intercede with Vadim in many things. And Olga has threatened Vadim: Leave me, and you'll never see your daughter again. But Sveta is her father's confidant too, the one to whom he pours out his heart, whom he has told all about me, trusting her not to repeat a word, and of course she does not. She would do anything to keep her parents together. She has promised her father that, no matter what happens, he will not lose her.

But it is only rarely that Sveta allows anything to interrupt her homework. She works hard at school and she knows what she is working toward: grades that will lead to a scholarship that will get her out of this place. If she must, she will stop her ears with her fingers. But sometimes she feels that she is only driving the curses and the screams deeper and deeper into her skull. Deep, they will echo for the rest of her life.

I could tell her.

➤

These are the first cool clear days of autumn. Vadim and I are still seeing each other, the same way we have always seen each other. On days when he is "lucky"—that is, getting a lot of fares—he calls me from a phone booth in the street to ask if he can visit. If I am home, I always say yes. We always make love as soon as he arrives, and I always come. Later we talk. Sometimes I try to offer him something to eat, but he never accepts. He says he isn't hungry, but I think maybe he doesn't trust my cooking. My lack of domestic skills is a source of wonder and amusement to him. He cannot believe how messy he sometimes finds the apartment. I have to work, I tell him. I don't have time to clean. "No," he says. "You are lazy. Russian women work, cook, clean, and take care of children—all." Russian women can do everything, and men (the proverb continues) can do the rest.

On unlucky days, when he has no time to spare, I sometimes meet him downstairs and walk or sit with him for a while, and we smoke and we talk. Sometimes when I come home from work I find him waiting in the cab outside my building. The night I said goodbye to him was one of those fall evenings that are so soft and fresh they could be evenings in spring. The sun has just gone down, and the sky is the same tender blush as a robin's breast. The streets are crowded with people on their way home from work. My own workday was long and hard, and it shows. Vadim notices right away how tired I look, as I get in the front seat. We kiss. His is a greedy, taking kind of kiss that always makes me feel as if he were sucking out some of my soul. He is in a good mood as usual, though he is tired too, and he has a headache: I can see it in his eyes. He is drinking a soda. He is wearing jeans and the same black sweater he was wearing the first day I ever saw him, the same sweater and jeans he wore every day to class. Like all my students: same clothes, day in, day out. His leather jacket is on the front seat between us; that's where he usually keeps the gun, under the jacket, but when I am in the cab he slips the gun under his seat.

I have aspirin in my bag and I offer him some, but he

won't take it. (A man must never complain to a woman that he is in pain, he once told me. Unchivalrous, I guess.) But you really should take some, I say. And we laugh, remembering an old exercise from class. "When you have a headache," one student said, "you should call forth the doctor."

"I must tell you what I saw today." Vadim is always full of stories. He sees the most incredible sights from his cab. Eighth Avenue: a woman, dazed on drugs, facing oncoming cars with one foot propped on top of a fire hydrant, her skirt hiked up to her hips, and "without anything under: you could see—all."

I teach him the word *hooker*. That is how our last conversation began. There were plenty of hookers in Odessa too, Vadim says, and sometimes he and Yuri would get in the car and go find one of them, and they would take her into the car, and she would have to satisfy them. He used those words: *have to satisfy*.

Some confusion here. Could hookers in Odessa be all that different from hookers in the rest of the world? "I don't understand. What do you mean, *have to*?"

Vadim looks puzzled, as if he thought his meaning was obvious. "She have to because—because she need this corner. This is where she work, how she make money."

"That's just the point." My voice comes out shrill. I feel a stirring at the roots of my hair. An abomination is looming. "Why didn't you have to pay her?"

The look on Vadim's face is familiar to me. He is afraid that it's his English that is the problem here, that once again he has been unable to make himself understood. I have seen that anxious look of his a thousand times. When he speaks again, his voice sounds dim and fuzzy to me, like the voice on an ancient recording. "Because I"—muttering in Russian, searching for the word—"beat?"

What is he trying to say? He beat her? Because he *did* beat her? Because he *would* beat her? How much depends on an auxiliary. "You beat her."

"No, no. I don't beat her. I don't have to beat, because she is not stupid, believe me. But she *think* I beat—oh, I am sorry. My English!"—gesturing deploringly at himself. "Do you understand?"

I nod my head yes and he grins, showing all his teeth. "You always could understand me."

I have closed my eyes, I cannot see his face, but I know that his look is anxious again. His hand cups my cheek. "Beloved, you are pale." He kisses me again and I close my eyes more tightly and think, Drowning must feel something like this.

He says, "You must go to rest now, and I to work."

But I have gotten my breath back and I have one more question. "Vadim, those girls—women—the hookers. Didn't they have any—protection?" Vadim looks baffled and I grope on: "Wasn't there someone—usually there is someone—some man—who—"

"Ah!" His brow clears and he slaps his thigh, as if he finally saw why I have been so slow to grasp things. "Yes, of course," he says. "You didn't understand me right. I *was* their protection."

He glances at his watch and swears in Russian. "My dear, I am sorry. You know I want to stay here with you forever, but I must go now, I must make money. Today I am very unlucky."

A police car streaks past, its siren piercing the dusk. Vadim winces and touches his fingers to his temple. With a sheepish look he says, "I think maybe you are right, my dear. Give me please this aspirin."

I take the bottle from my bag and shake out two tablets. I hold them out to him and rapidly swallow and blink back tears as he bows his large head over my hand and eats from my palm. He washes the aspirin down with the last of the soda he has been drinking and tosses the can out the window. Clankety-clank-clank-clank. In that hollow, tinny sound I hear the rhythms of a snickering laugh.

I get out of the cab and Vadim covers the half-block to the traffic light in a breath, scattering jaywalkers with blasts of his horn.

The soda can has rolled under a parked car. I have to go down on my knees to get at it. Stopped at the light up ahead, Vadim must be able to see me in his mirror. I imagine how I must look to him; I imagine him grinning and shaking his head. The light changes then and he takes off. I stand there holding the empty can and I watch him speed away, speeding out of my life without even knowing it—as he never really knew anything about me.

That night as I was crying in bed, I imagined that he— who else but he?—was there to comfort me. "It is life in Odessa." It is life everywhere.

He let me go quietly, accepting my story that I had to leave town for a couple of weeks and that I would call him when I got back. And when I never called he did not pursue me. "Is better this way," I heard him saying to himself. (As if he talked to himself in broken English.)

How bad did he have to be? What did he have to do? I never told anyone the end of this story.

One day, months later, something went wrong with my answering machine, which played back old messages I thought had long been erased. "I know what means *actually* now!"

And for a long time after, whenever I was in the street, I would look so hard and searchingly at passing cabs that often a driver would slow down and stop for me, thinking I was a fare.

❦

They say the thing most feared always happens, but I told myself it was too unlikely, it never would, not in a hundred years. But only two years passed before it did.

Bad weather, a late day at work, friends waiting in a bar—I stepped into the street and raised my arm.

He came at me so fast, shooting diagonally across Sixth Avenue to the din of brakes and horns, that I jumped back onto the curb.

"Hello, my teacher!"

When I got in the front seat, expressing my astonishment, he replied that there was really no cause for astonishment: "I am in this neighborhood many times a day."

He looked good. He had put on weight. Less thin, he looked healthier, and he had a decent haircut.

A hint of umbrage as I buckled my seat belt. "You think I don't know how to drive?"

During the ride uptown, he never stopped smoking or talking. He had moved to the new apartment that he had wanted. He had borrowed the money to buy the lease from his wife's brother, and he had already paid much of it back. "If you could see where I lived before," he said, "and if you could see where I live now, you would know that I am really doing all right for myself." Only he and his wife and daughter had moved to the new apartment. He was especially pleased about that.

He was working six days a week now, earning a little over two hundred dollars a day. After paying for gas and seventy-five dollars to the owner of the cab, he had about a hundred dollars left for himself. His wife was working too, taking care of a sick old man a few mornings a week for six dollars an hour. Things between him and Olga were just the same. "She will never change," he says. But he is smiling as he says it. (Like a dog on *hay*, not on harvest, I have learned the saying goes. A dog in the manger.)

I want to know about his daughter.

"She will go to NYU. This is a very good university." (Perhaps I had never heard of it.) "She says now she wants to be a lawyer, but she is still young. We will see. And she has a boyfriend, a very nice boy—American." He shrugs. "But she is not really serious about boys now, my daughter. She thinks only about school. Russian girls marry young and have children right away. When I first came here I thought Americans were crazy because they didn't do the same. But now I see it is much better the American way. I am glad for my daughter. She will be happier.

"I like this boyfriend, but before him she had another boyfriend, and I didn't like him. He was a very bad person. I threw him out of the apartment one time. I kicked him all the way down the stairs. And that was something, believe me, because, you see, I live on the seventeenth floor." (Teeth.) "But my daughter is doing very well. And her English!" He rolls his eyes admiringly and we go through a red light. I myself have been admiring how, though his accent is as thick as I remembered it, Vadim has yet to make any mistakes.

I want to know about drugs. Is he still shooting up? He looks almost surprised at the question. "I don't do it anymore—not for a long time now. I am too old for this, and besides, it is very dangerous here. I don't trust the drugs they sell here. I don't trust black people. And you have to worry about AIDS. What a country. We don't have AIDS in Russia," he misinforms me. I start to tell him, but he insists: "In Odessa I never heard of this thing." Another red light.

We have almost reached my destination when he asks, "And what about you, my dear? I thought about you a lot all this time."

In two years much in my life has changed. I don't live in the same apartment, I don't have the same job, and I have a new (American) boyfriend. But here we are, my friends are waiting, and I know that Vadim is not really interested in any of this. The only thing I mention is that I am going to China.

"China?" He seems unimpressed. "Why do you want to go there?"

I tell him that I have taken a job. I will be teaching English in Shanghai. "I have friends who've done it. They say it's hard but fascinating."

Vadim looks doubtful. "Maybe. But I don't like Chinese people."

I never told him. He never asked. I tell him now.

He has stopped the cab, and we are sitting turned toward each other. I had noticed right away when I got in the cab that there was no jacket on the front seat. I don't know where the gun is, but I am aware that for the entire ride I have sat as if it were lying right there between us.

"Really?" says Vadim, but he doesn't look very surprised. That was one of the things about Vadim: Nothing in life appeared to surprise him.

"I didn't know," he says. "I didn't see it." He cocks his head and narrows his eyes, trying to see it now. "And mother?" When I tell him he nods and says, "When two races marry, the daughter will be pretty. It is the same with my girl. But that is the only good thing about this kind of marriage, believe me."

He cocks his head to the other side then and says, "Why did you run away from me?" And before I can speak he answers for me. "You were afraid. I know it. But why?" More than a hint of umbrage now. "I am not a bad person. You had to know I would never hurt you. I was always very careful with you."

Often when he came to see me, as soon as he stepped through the door he would kiss me, and as he was kissing me he would reach down and gather me up into his arms. He would hold me for a long time, hugging me to his chest, kissing me, and then start walking with me into the apartment, to the bedroom, to the bed.

"My friends are waiting," I say. "I have to go."

Of course he will not let me pay him. Does he still cheat his passengers? I wonder, as I get out of the cab.

"May I call you, my dear?" His tone is affectionate,

insinuating, full of humor. Twisting his mouth to blow smoke out of the corner. My skin remembers him.

"No," I say, and at this Vadim looks many things at once: a little wounded, a little bemused, a little mocking, and, as always, a little sorry for me.

"In that case, okay, goodbye again." Not a man to ask twice. Lots of fish in the sea. He drives off, calling, "Take it easy, my dear!"

Did I mention the weather? Cold rain and a spiteful wind that first helps me get my umbrella up, then tries to tear it away from me.

My friends are waiting. They are waiting inside the bar right there on the corner, but I hesitate, as if I didn't know which way to go. Or I made it all up: There was no one waiting for me, and now I would catch another cab and go home.

Of course he was bad. He was very bad. A brute. A pimp. A menace to women. I know why he pitied me.

And it isn't true that I never saw him angry. He became angry with me when he saw that I was afraid, especially if there were other people around. For example, one night, walking in the park, the way I kept looking over my shoulder made him very angry. He took hold of my wrists and he shook me. "I told you: You don't have to be afraid when you are with me. If I have to fight for you, I fight. If I have to die for you, I die. I cannot do differently. Differently, I am not man."

I think he was a good father to his daughter.

❧

At different times in my life I have made up my mind to try therapy. It seemed an obvious thing to do. Everyone else was doing it. Women, especially, swore by it. Perhaps I was just wildly unlucky, but the male doctors turned out to be easy to seduce, and I didn't fare much better with the women. The last one I tried had told me at the end of our first session, "A background like that, no wonder you're here. You don't know *who* you are!" Then she added, more to herself than to me: "Still, there must have been something good back there: It must have come from the father."

I thought she should not have said that.

I even took someone's advice and sought out that rarity, a Chinese-American therapist, who kept exhorting me to summon more rage to our sessions, as if rage were a dog I could whistle into the room. *Here, Rage!* (But my mother, seen as the root of so much trouble, lived in a state of constant rage, and what good had come of that? A question for which Dr. Wu had no answer.)

When I was in college, I had a friend who insisted on going home with me one holiday. This was a woman from an ethereally privileged world who prided herself on her lack of prejudice. The idea of visiting a housing project excited her. I suppose it seemed romantic and daring. Throughout her visit she was very polite, but I could tell that she was nervous. Later, I heard from others the report she gave of her visit, as if it had been to a sideshow: how scary it was and how weird she found my family; how she couldn't sleep at night on the cheap cot that had been pulled out for her. I remained friends with her (some sort of twisted pride, I think), but I never forgave her. Some time after the visit she said to me, "And how are your little parents?" It was the closest I ever came to punching anyone. Now, that was rage.

It would not have occurred to me to introduce Vadim to my friends. Although they wanted to hear all about him and to see the photographs, they would not have liked to meet him; it didn't matter how much Pushkin he could recite. Some saw the whole affair as a kind of backsliding on my part. ("You can take the girl out of the projects, but . . . ")

There are people who will tell you that, no matter what you achieve in life or what opportunities come your way, you must stick with your own class. To try to rise above your class is to betray it and to risk losing your soul.

After my father died I had a nervous breakdown. It may have been the illness, or it may have been the medication used to treat the illness, but I lost what had been a very good memory. Before the breakdown I could, if I wished, turn to some scene from the past and run it like a movie in my head. I could bring it all back: where the scene had taken place, what kind of day it was, what clothes people were wearing, the expressions on their faces, entire conversations word for word. It may have been the price of cure, but it was a hard adjustment for me, becoming a person with ordinary powers of memory.

It was only recently, when I read somewhere that there are seven million Changs in the world, that I remembered this: I had a classmate named Joey Chang, one of the very few Asians in our grade school. I must have told him about my father, and he must have told his parents, who called immediately to invite our family to a barbecue. This invitation caused some consternation in our household. Remember: We were not used to going out. And we had no car, so we would have to take the bus. But there'd be no leaving my father home *this* time.

Joey Chang had two little siblings, a girl and a boy. As we sat eating spareribs, these two were all over my father, climbing into his lap, swinging from his arms, until finally he gave up trying to eat and let them drag him off. For the rest of the afternoon he played with them nearby on the lawn.

We did not return the Changs' invitation, and they did not invite us to their house again. I could imagine Joey's parents saying to him after we left: "They aren't really Chinese!"

Back home from the barbecue, my sisters and I were downcast. "He never played like that with *us*." A revelation and a shock, that brief glimpse of a happy, active father. Our mother didn't see anything shocking about it. "Ach, such adorable little Chinese kids—what do you expect? You have to forgive him. I would probably be the same with little German children."

Some things it would be death to forgive.

"Why did you want to hurt yourself?" asked the doctor who admitted me into the hospital.

"Why did you go with this man? What did you want?" The doctor sitting across from me now is a woman. A stout, shapeless, housemother-type, with a homely manner of speaking and an even homelier face. I look at that face and think: How can she possibly understand? This woman has never been ravished.